BEHIND THE PRETTY PINK DOOR

HAVE YOU MET THE NEW NEIGHBOURS YET?

M J HARDY

Copyrighted Material

Copyright © M J Hardy 2020

M J Hardy has asserted her rights under the Copyright, Designs and Patents Act 1988 to be identified as the Author of this work.

This book is a work of fiction and except in the case of historical fact, any resemblance to actual persons, living or dead, is purely coincidental.
All rights reserved. No part of this book may be reproduced or transmitted in any form without written permission of the author, except by a reviewer who may quote brief passages for review purposes only.

<u>This book uses UK spelling</u>

MORE BOOKS BY M J HARDY

M J Hardy
EXPECT THE UNEXPECTED

The Girl on Gander Green Lane
    The Husband Thief
    Living the Dream
    The Woman who Destroyed Christmas
    The Grey Woman

You're Invited!

Join my Newsletter
Follow me on Facebook

BEHIND THE PRETTY PINK DOOR

M J Hardy

What's going on behind the pretty pink door?

Can something so pretty hide a dreadful truth?

Esme and Lucas thought they had moved up in the world.

They bought an impressive new house on a desirable development but do they fit in?

Nancy and Adrian moved to escape a secret they appear to have packed and brought with them.

What will the neighbours think if they discover what it is?

Jasmine and Liam seem to have it all. Their neighbours want what they have but would they go as far to achieve it?

Then there's Keith and Sandra Wickham who everyone wishes hadn't moved there at all.

They all have one thing in common and it's not the street they moved into.

It's their fascination for what goes on behind the pretty pink door.

Who lives there and what secrets does it hide?

Secrets have a habit of coming out and none of theirs are safe.

What happens when the pretty pink door opens and lets them all inside?

Sometimes it's easier to turn a blind eye than to face the consequences but true evil is found in the ones who look away and do nothing.

PROLOGUE

LOLA

*I*f I hide under the bed will it all go away?

I wish I had that option because anything is better than this.

The sound of the car pulling up outside makes my heart thump and my nerves tingle. My father looks at me and the ruin in his eyes will live with me forever. It's all there in that look. Pain, guilt, despair, love… I could go on.

His voice breaks. "I'm sorry."

"It will be ok."

At some point in this, the child in me grew up and our roles reversed. He needs me to make it better because he is drowning, choking and dying inside.

I smile bravely through my tears as the sound of two car doors slamming bring reality to our door.

This is a pivotal point in both our lives, and even breathing is difficult. I want to run; I want to hide and I want to make everything better—but I can't. This is it, how it must be—for now, anyway.

"I'll sort it, you must believe that."

"Don't." My voice is soft and disguises how I really feel. I'm angry and hurt and so worried I can't think straight. There is so much to say, but only one thing matters.

"I love you."

He turns sharply and the look in his eyes strips me bare. I need to hold it together and so smile bravely through my tears, "I'll be ok."

The footsteps are close to our door, they are like a drumbeat counting down the last moments of a life that was never perfect but normal to me—to us.

Father and daughter, getting by together. Not anymore, not until things change, so with a heavy heart, I walk towards the only person I love and smile through my tears. "I love you dad, please stay safe."

His arms wrap around me and hold me close, and I almost stop breathing. A thousand words I should say spin around my mind, but none of them gets a voice. They have no power anyway because this is how it is and as my father crushes me to him, I feel his emotion tearing at my soul. If this is the last time I hold my father, I want it to count. I want to remember how I feel at this moment because that will get me through. I need to be strong and I need to be brave because we will get through this and blink in the sunlight on the other side. Life will carry on and we will leave this behind us and never speak of it again.

The loud knock on the door causes my heart to race and for a fraction of a second, time stands still. My father's arms tighten around me and I wonder what's going through his mind right now.

Then he breaks away and says almost gruffly, "I'm sorry, Lola."

He breaks away and only the dull sound of his boot on the bare floor gives life to a room where two hearts stopped beating one hour ago. Is it possible to live when your heart ceased working? Apparently, it is because we are proof of that. Sixty minutes ago, our lives changed and I wasn't prepared for how much, however as his hand finds the door handle, I know I must dig deep because what happens next determines our future.

CHAPTER 1

ESME

"Lucas, don't you dare let that cat out."

The door slams and I feel my nerves fraying by the second as I see Pixie scurrying down the driveway towards the house opposite.

Quickly, I check for cars before racing down the stairs two steps at a time and flinging open the door.

"Pixie, come here, girl."

I may as well be talking to myself because she's gone. In the brief few moments that it took to make the transition from upstairs window to path in front of the door, she's disappeared and I look at my husband crossly as he unloads yet another cardboard box from the rental van.

"Did you forget to pack your common sense?"

"What?" He looks annoyed and I take a deep breath. "Pixie, the cat, remember?"

"What about her?"

"Honestly Lucas, we spoke about this. We agreed she was to be kept inside for at least a week to get used to her new home and now you've ruined what was supposed to be a textbook operation."

"What are you talking about?"

"Settling Pixie into her new home, remember. The vet and the internet agree that cats should be kept indoors because it's likely she'll be confused and try to find our old home. She will be disorientated, upset and worried and unable to find her way back to us. You'll have to stop what you're doing and help me find her."

"Stop what I'm doing, are you crazy? This van is only ours for one more hour before I have to return it, unless you want to pay the penalty."

"Weigh it up, darling, and think about the penalty you will pay if my baby goes missing and never returns. The penalty you will pay will be far more costly than a late fee for returning a van that was never big enough in the first place. Honestly, I wonder why I married you sometimes."

"Good afternoon."

Looking up, I see a woman standing at the end of our driveway, smiling at us with a hint of amusement in her eyes. Feeling as if I've been caught fighting in the playground by the teacher, I say quickly, "Oh, hi."

She nods to Lucas, who smiles politely and then puts the box down and heads her way. I join him and the woman holds out her hand.

"I'm pleased to meet you, I'm your neighbour Nancy."

"Oh, how lovely, I'm Esme and this is my husband Lucas."

I look with interest at my new friend because I'm in no doubt we will be. It's what happens when you move next door to someone in places like these. You forge an instant connection and I can see us sharing many coffees over the breakfast bar as we put the world to rights.

She smiles politely and waves her hand in the direction of the house beside ours.

"Yes, we moved in last month, I think we were the second ones here. Only Sandra and Keith were here before us, but

Jasmine and Liam weren't close behind. Goodness, I can't keep up with it all."

Looking around with interest, once again I feel the smug contentment of someone who thinks she has it all. Yes, this was always going to be a good move for us, a step up and the chance to mingle with the middle classes where I have always aspired to be.

"So, Nancy, what's it like living here, any advice?"

"Oh, you'll find out, it can be a bit intense actually but in a nice way. I was going to call in later on this evening with a 'welcome to your new home' bottle of wine and card, but I was passing and couldn't resist saying hi."

Once again, she smiles and then says quickly, "Anyway, I'll leave you to it because I know what it's like on moving day. If you need anything I'm only next door and Adrian, my husband, can always provide a strong pair of arms if you need any heavy lifting done and if he can't, I have a son who I would welcome you dragging from his computer games for five seconds to do some actual physical activity for once."

She smiles and heads off and I turn to Lucas and grin. "Well, she seems nice, I told you it would be ok."

Shrugging, he leans down and lifts the box, grumbling, "Why do you always put that false voice on when you meet people, it's embarrassing?"

"What do you mean, I always speak like that?"

I whisper it furiously hoping nobody hears and he shakes his head. "Yes, you do. Suddenly, you've become some la-de-da lady and we both know that's not you, Esme, why do you always feel the need to make out you are something you're not?"

Feeling like kicking the box across the bloody driveway, I just turn and storm inside, completely forgetting why I came out here in the first place.

I retreat to the kitchen and look around with increasing

panic as I see the mammoth task waiting for me. This kitchen is bigger than our old one so everything should fit in, but at the moment it looks as if it will take some doing, so I sigh in defeat and flick the kettle on instead. This can wait because a nice cup of tea is taking priority right now over anything else, and I'm almost tempted not to offer Lucas any.

Fake voice, I don't know where he gets these ideas from.

By the time Lucas has emptied the van, I'm beginning to lose the will to live. I thought this would be easy. We didn't have much to bring anyway, preferring to buy new when we got here, but this is overwhelming.

A knock at the door distracts me from the cardboard mountain and I head towards it with interest, taking a moment to enjoy the sound of a doorbell that actually works for a change, unlike our old one that was always out of batteries.

As I open the door, a flash of black races past me and I feel the relief hit me, "Pixie."

My runaway baby has returned and I can sleep tonight, but as I look up, I see she didn't return alone. A man is standing there holding an envelope and he regards me with interest.

"Good afternoon, I hope you don't mind the intrusion, but I'm Keith Wickham, the coordinator of the Meadow Vale housing committee and wanted to welcome you personally."

"I'm pleased to meet you; I'm Esme and my husband Lucas is just out for a bit, but he won't be long."

"That's fine, I just wanted to drop in some information you may need, you know the sort of thing, bin collection times, nearest shop, pub, etc."

"That's great, thank you, I appreciate it."

He nods as he hands me the envelope and I see him look past me and feel immediately on edge at the state of the house.

"Hm, we nearly bought this house, but the sun was in the wrong position for Sandra, she wanted a south facing garden but this one's north."

"Oh, we don't care about things like that."

I feel a little defensive because he throws me one of those looks that's loaded with pity and I say quickly, "Well, thank you again, I appreciate it."

Hoping he will take the hint, I make to close the door but he says quickly, "Oh yes, I saw you have a cat. You may want to keep it in for a bit. There are quite a few of them around and can get very territorial to newcomers."

Despite the fact that was my plan all along, I resent a total stranger telling me what to do and say evenly, "Thank you, so, um, Keith, which house is yours?"

He waves across the road and my heart sinks as he says with pride, "Ours is the Wisteria design, Sandra always demands the best, so of course we had to go for the most expensive."

"Lucky Sandra." I smile, but inside I'm groaning. Could this man be any more boring if he tried? In fact, I am definitely not picturing any cosy get together with this couple. If I did, I may shoot myself.

He looks around and I feel myself cringing with embarrassment as his gaze falls to our rather old Nissan Micra that has seen better days. His own Mercedes sits gleaming on his driveway, and I know enough about cars to know that one must have cost a small fortune.

Trying to distract him from stripping anymore of my self-worth, I say quickly, "I met Nancy earlier, she seems nice."

"Yes, Nancy and Adrian are the kind of people you want as neighbours, you know the sort, upstanding members of the community who are not afraid to get involved. I'm hoping you and your husband are out of the same mould."

"Of course, we are keen to dive head first into life at Meadow Vale. We can't wait, actually."

Keith just smiles, "Well, I must be off. A game of golf beckons. Do you play golf, or your husband perhaps?"

Another sinking feeling highlights my increasing list of failings and I say quietly, "No, I'm afraid we don't. We were thinking of taking it up though."

The look he gives me tells me even he knows this is a lie because I'm sure that if I even mentioned it to Lucas, he would shoot me down in flames. He's always hated golf and can't begin to understand why anyone would enjoy hitting a ball with a stick and wearing crazy checked trousers. Hopefully we won't have much to do with Keith Wickham, anyway.

CHAPTER 2

ESME

The door slams and my heart sinks. Here we go.

"Mum, where are you?"

"In here."

Seeing them racing into the room, I have to smile as I see the excitement in the eyes of Billy and Archie, my two boys who are the spitting image of their father.

"Wow, this place is huge."

I take a moment to gaze around with satisfaction because yes, this place is two steps up from our previous house in London. It's got more space, more rooms and more kerb appeal than the shabby terraced house we used to live in in Streatham. I still can't believe that we sold that house for so much money, enabling us to buy this much bigger one nearer the south coast. Luckily, Streatham house prices went through the roof when commuters decided they wanted to settle there and regenerate an area that had seen better days. We were allocated the house by the council and bought it a few years back on 'the right to buy' scheme and have never looked back. So, here we are in Meadow Vale, living the high life and giving our kids the best start in life.

"Can I choose my room?"

"I want to choose, why does he get to go first?"

The boys argue almost immediately and I snap, "I chose your rooms. In fact, your things are already there, so I'll leave it up to you to find them."

They are out of the door almost immediately, and I hear their footsteps thundering up the stairs and sigh. Boys are very challenging in a lot of ways, but I wouldn't change them for the world. Two gorgeous mirror images of their father who need a firm hand because they're at that age where they could go either way. It was quite a timely move because they were forming friendships with the wrong boys and I could see trouble in their future. Billy is due to start secondary school in September and the one he was allocated is one of the roughest in the area. Now they have a place at local schools they can walk to that were both rated as outstanding by Ofsted. Yes, this move came just in the nick of time and I'm determined to make it a good one. We will make sure we fit in here because it's time to change direction and make something of our lives.

"I could murder a cup of tea."

Lucas throws his keys on the counter and looks so tired I feel a little bad. He's worked so hard to make this happen and I know he was against moving out of London to the country because he's lived in Streatham all his life.

Walking over, I wrap my arms around him and whisper, "Thank you."

As his arms fold me inside the familiar, I breathe easier. We may argue and he may annoy me most of the time, but I wouldn't be without him. He is everything to me and I want him to know that.

"I love you, babe."

His voice whispers the words that always mean so much,

and I squeeze him a little tighter. "Me too, you know we've made the right decision, don't you?"

"If you're happy, I'm happy."

Pulling back, I stare at the familiar face that I've loved since I first set eyes on it in the playground at Streatham High fifteen years ago and grin. "I wonder what our friends will make of this place?"

"They'll think we've gone posh, sold out and joined the white-collar brigade."

"You're probably right, but you don't regret it, do you?"

I feel a little anxious because I nagged him for months to move here. As soon as I had the idea, I ran like a sprinter with it. It became the most important thing in my life to move out of London to a place I thought would be safe, respectable and the sort of community you see on the television. Nothing bad ever happens in places like these and I say softly, "Listen."

He looks up and I laugh at the puzzled frown that he wears so well, "What?"

"Silence. Lovely, blissful silence. No traffic, no sirens and no shouting."

I look past him through the patio doors onto a garden that is double the size of our last one and my heart settles. This was the best decision we ever made and even the loud thump on the ceiling and the sound of arguing doesn't dampen my spirits because I know we made the right decision. We are home.

"I'll go."

Lucas rolls his eyes as we hear the boys fighting, and we share an amused grin. They are always fighting, but I know it's just what brothers do. They've always been the same, but they love each other just as fiercely. Luckily, they are close in age with just eighteen months separating them and do everything together. I just hope they don't show me up because I want us to fit in here. I want to live the life I always thought respectable people do, and I want us to be accepted.

Lucas heads off to deal with the boys and I make them a snack. Lucas picked them up from school after dropping the van back to the rental company, and the time that took gave me a few hours to get some order to a kitchen that I only dreamed of owning. It's not the most expensive house on the development, but was the only one we could afford. Four bedrooms and a huge open-plan kitchen diner with an ensuite that I can't wait to experience. Our last house had three bedrooms if you can call one of them a bedroom, more like an enlarged cupboard. No, now we have a spare room for guests and my Pinterest board is full of images of exactly how this house will look just as soon as I can persuade Lucas to step up and do a spot of decorating. I can't wait to show our family and friends just how far we've come, and they will be astonished at how much more we got for our money here in Meadow Vale.

By the time the boys make it downstairs, I feel as if I've settled in already and as we sit around the table eating the makeshift tea I hastily prepared, I try to reassure everyone that this was what we all wanted.

"So, what do you think?"

I look at the boys hopefully and Billy shrugs. "I prefer our old house."

Archie nods. "Me too. This place is weird."

Lucas grins as I say crossly, "Don't be silly, this place is heaps better than our old house, you've got your own rooms for one thing."

Lucas nods. "And a bigger garden. I could rig up your goals and you could play football out there."

I stare at him in horror, "Over my dead body, there's a playing field two minutes away, they can go there."

"Can we have a trampoline?"

Archie looks at me hopefully and I nod. "Of course, we'll check the Argos catalogue later, maybe they deliver."

Lucas groans. "For god's sake, Esme, we've been here two minutes and you've started already. Couldn't you wait at least a week before you give me one more job to do?"

"If you think I've only got one job for you, you're mistaken. The list is growing by the second."

The boys laugh as Lucas groans and I laugh lightly. Yes, this is what I imagined. Us all sitting around the table sharing family time in a place we can grow and breathe fresh air. I knew we'd made the right decision.

CHAPTER 3

ESME

*A*fter a sub-standard tea, we go for a walk to escape even more unpacking and as I walk hand-in-hand with Lucas, the boys' race ahead.

"I already love it here, we're so lucky."

Lucas nods. "It's quiet though, I'm not sure if I'll ever get used to not hearing the noise of the traffic. It feels a little eerie if I'm honest."

"It's better, way better because noise pollution is a silent danger."

"Silent danger, what on earth are you talking about? How can noise pollution be a silent danger?"

Lucas laughs as I say crossly, "What I mean, is that you don't notice it's a problem because you've become immune to it. Now it's gone, you notice it, which means you're better off."

Lucas laughs beside me and I mumble, "Well, I know what I mean."

He squeezes my hand. "Yes, only you know what goes on in that brain of yours."

As we pass, I look with interest at the houses that are

similar to ours but a little different in some ways. There were four types of house built here, and each has its own name. The Wisteria is the most expensive with five bedrooms and three bathrooms and a rather impressive layout downstairs. Then there's the Dahlia which has four bedrooms and a separate dining room with a smaller kitchen. The Daisy is a three-storey town house with an impressive master suite on the top floor and then there's ours, the Rose, a four-bedroom home with smaller rooms and one less bathroom. The garden is also slightly smaller, but more than enough for us. We also only have a single garage whereas the two more expensive ones have double garages, but never having had the luxury of one before, we are more than happy with a single. In Streatham we were lucky to find a space in the road outside our house, so this is pure luxury.

As we walk, I look with interest at the houses that surround ours and feel smug as I look at how high we climbed. We've made it, we're now living the dream and I know we made the right decision, despite what Lucas thinks.

My husband is unusually quiet beside me, and I know he feels out of sorts. He was content to stay in London, I suppose because it's all he's ever known—all we've ever known, and yet he did this for me.

I squeeze his hand, feeling so grateful I found him. Everyone thought we were young and foolish when we got engaged at sixteen. When we married at seventeen, I could see the resigned expressions on both sets of parent's faces as they thought we had made a huge mistake and yet here we are, twenty years later and still going strong with two gorgeous boys and a house I never dreamed of owning. We worked hard for it though, and it certainly hasn't been easy. I mean, there were a few speed bumps along the way that slowed us down. A few redundancies and missed opportunities and the fact it took us a few failed attempts to get the family we craved so much.

The tears burn as I think about the dark time when getting pregnant was the most important thing in my life. It consumed me and I couldn't understand why I was unsuccessful. I checked out medically and so did Lucas, but through no lack of trying, it never happened. It made little sense and I suppose I became a little obsessed with it but it paid off in the end. The results are play fighting a short distance away and I shout, "Boys, stop fighting, behave yourselves."

Lucas laughs softly, "They'll never change."

"They'll have to, I mean, I'm pretty sure this place frowns upon children."

"Now you're being ridiculous."

"Am I though? I told you before, this place is eerily silent. Look around you Lucas, where are the kids on bikes? Where are the windows open with music blaring out and where are the kids playing? Come to think of it, I don't think I've seen any children all the times we looked around. Do you think there are any, or is it just people like Keith and Sandra Wickham, maybe our boys are the only life in the place?"

"Who are Keith and Sandra Wickham when they're at home?"

"Our new neighbours and he is seriously square. He popped over when you were picking up the boys and gave me a folder on things we need to know. He was a little straight and above himself but maybe I was just being harsh, I mean, it was kind of him to stop by, don't you think?"

Lucas nods and falls silent, and I kick myself. Why did I plant one more seed of doubt in his mind? He never wanted to move, and the boys certainly didn't. In fact, they told me on numerous occasions I was ruining their lives and they would hate me forever. I didn't care, mother knows best and yet now we're here I'm not so sure. Was this the right move? It had better be.

As we walk around the corner, I look at the houses with interest. They built this part of the development before ours and it subsequently has a more lived-in look. Pretty houses set around the village green that have beautiful flower gardens and established borders. Lucas is quiet beside me and I whisper, "Do you wish we lived in this part?"

He sighs and says somewhat irritably, "No I don't, Esme. I'm happy with what we've got and so should you. Anyway, these houses weren't available, you know that."

"Oh, for goodness' sake, Lucas, I'm only asking, why are you so irritable?"

As we walk, I feel annoyed that he's in one of his moods. I know we should be doing a million things back at the house like hanging curtains and settling in, but I was keen for us to take a breath and discover the area we moved to.

Meadow Vale is split into two parts at the moment. The first phase of houses set around a pretty green and then the part we have moved into, a smart street around the corner of the green. Houses were in demand and we were lucky to find a buyer for ours so quickly and I have to pinch myself that we pulled it off. There is more building work to come and I hope it doesn't alter the ambience of the place because now it's perfect. However, as we walk, it strikes me how deserted this place is. There are quite a few houses here, but no movement or activity. No eager husbands mowing the lawn or tinkering with their cars. In fact, there are very few cars around and I can only suppose they are at work, or the cars are safely locked in the garages of the smart houses.

After a while, I whisper, "Can you feel it?"

"What?"

"Oh, I don't know, maybe I'm being stupid."

"Just tell me." Lucas is irritated and I almost say nothing

but whisper, "I've just got a strange feeling we're being watched."

He laughs softly and squeezes my hand. "We probably are. I'm guessing the neighbours are curious about the new arrivals. I'm sure it won't take you long to infiltrate the development. By the time I return home from work one day, you will have all the gossip and tell me things I'd really rather not know."

"Maybe you're right but I don't know, something feels off to me."

"Boys, if I have to tell you one more time, you'll go to your rooms with no tea."

"Supper, Lucas."

"What?"

He looks at me in surprise and I whisper, "I expect they call it supper here. Don't make us stand out any more than we do already."

I can tell I've said the wrong thing when Lucas says tightly, "Stop."

"What?"

"This, pretending we're something we're not. We've always said tea and I'm not about to change just to fit in with people we don't even know. For all you know, these people could be murderers, gangsters, drug addicts or wife beaters. Don't be so quick to think they are better than us."

"Don't be ridiculous, of course nobody here is like that. We are in a respectable neighbourhood now and have left all that behind in Streatham."

"Are you serious?"

Lucas looks at me with disapproval and I colour up a little. "Ok, maybe I'm being unfair on our friends back home but honestly Lucas, do you really think Meadow Vale is home to riff raff? Just look at the number of windows with shutters on them, that should tell you these people have taste and money."

"Or something to hide."

"Now you stop. In fact, I want shutters as a matter of urgency and we have absolutely nothing to hide except for the mess you boys make."

Sighing heavily, Lucas shouts, "Come on guys, time to head back."

I know not to push my luck any further and just fall into step beside my husband but I know how I feel, something is off about this place and I'm certain we are being watched, call it a sixth sense, I can feel it.

CHAPTER 4

ESME

A knock on the door the next morning takes me by surprise and upon opening it, find the smiling woman from next door holding an envelope and a bottle of wine.

"Good morning, I'm sorry to disturb you."

"Oh, no problem, would you like to come in?"

I feel a little flustered because as usual our house is a complete mess and I try not to let my relief show when she shakes her head and says apologetically, "I'm sorry, I can't stop. I'm heading off to Pilates, but I just wanted to welcome you officially and invite you around this evening for social drinks."

She hands me the bottle and the envelope and I smile gratefully. "That sounds great, we would love to come. What time?"

"Oh, shall we say seven? I've invited a few of the other neighbours and you can meet everyone in one go. Not that there's many of us—yet, but it's a start at least."

"Thank you, we would love to come."

With a smile and a wave, she heads back down the path

and I close the door feeling excited. Yes, this is just what I envisaged when we moved here. Drinks with neighbours, get-togethers and cosy chats over coffee. Now all we need is to find the local pub so Lucas will be happy and some friends for the boys.

"Who was that?"

Lucas materialises from the garden and I say happily, "Nancy from next door. They have invited us around there for social drinks at seven. I told you we'd fit right in."

"What the hell are social drinks when they're at home?"

Lucas raises his eyes and looks so shocked it makes me laugh. "The clue is in the title, babe, people here obviously like to party so you should fit right in."

"What about the boys, are they invited?"

"She didn't say."

Lucas shrugs, "Oh well, it's only next door, they can always stay here and shout if they need us."

He heads off upstairs to drill yet another hole, and I feel good about things. Social drinks, whatever next.

AT SEVEN ON THE DOT, we ring the doorbell next door and I smooth down my dress feeling anxious. Am I overdressed, will I fit in, will they be our sort of people?

Nancy answers the door with a huge smile, making me feel instantly at home and says sweetly, "Welcome, welcome, come on in and meet the others."

The noise of conversation stills as we walk into her kitchen that runs the length of the house at the back, and I feel strangely shy as I grip Lucas's hand and smile around me. Nancy pulls a man forward who nods with interest, "Hi, I'm Adrian, Nancy's husband, you must be Esme and Lucas, I'm pleased to meet you."

We shake his hand and Nancy says brightly, "This is Jasmine, she lives in the house opposite me and this is her husband Liam."

I look with interest at a slightly serious looking couple who nod politely and shake our hands. Jasmine looks to be in her late thirties, early forties and Liam looks a little older. They are both very smart and make me regret wearing the dress I bought from the well-known chain store when I see hers is more designer than budget brand. Liam is wearing smart chinos with a polo shirt and I don't miss the Rolex he has on his wrist. Both of them look immaculate and my heart sinks as I wonder what they must think of us.

Lucas nods and to everyone else he looks at ease, but I know he is hating every minute of this. He's never been one for social gatherings and this one's with strangers. He's a little uncomfortable talking to a room full of people he doesn't know, and I guess he's struggling.

My heart sinks when Keith Wickham steps forward, pulling a short, rather plump woman with him, which I'm guessing must be his wife Sandra. She is dressed in floral chiffon and her perfume reaches me before she does.

She looks to be in her early sixties and her make-up hasn't evolved because she's wearing bright blue eye shadow and her lips are painted pale pink and the blusher on her cheeks resembles a circus clown. She has more scarves draped around her than a belly dancer, and as she steps forward, I see her gaze stripping me bare. I shrink under it because it's obvious Sandra Wickham is the sort of woman who judges a person on sight.

"Welcome, welcome, allow me to introduce my wife Sandra."

Sandra looks so puffed up with her own importance I stifle a grin because Keith couldn't look any prouder than he does and I'm guessing she is used to being treated like a queen. In their house, anyway.

"I'm pleased to meet you both. You must tell me all about yourselves, I'm dying to know."

I open my mouth to speak but she interrupts, "We live in the house opposite, the Wisteria, you know, the big one."

My heart sinks as I nod politely.

"Anything you want to know just ask us because Keith prides himself on getting stuck into the community and giving something back."

"Yes - he said."

I daren't look at Lucas because I'm guessing if I did, the look he gives me would kill me on the spot.

Sandra carries on firing out words like a lethal machine gun.

"So, let me bring you up to speed."

She lowers her voice and leans in. "Watch out for that one over there."

I look to where her sharp gaze is pointing and see Jasmine looking as bored as Lucas undoubtedly is.

"She's a bit standoffish, which doesn't work well in a community like ours. Won't even put her name down for cricket club teas. Never volunteers for litter picking duty and won't entertain attending one of my community suppers. There's a story there though, mark my words."

I look at Jasmine and see a woman who I like on the spot because any woman who could rebuff Sandra goes up in my estimation.

"Look at her husband, I'm guessing he's a bit of a cad."

I almost spit out the wine I'm downing fast as Lucas goes still beside me.

"Dresses like a right player and the look in her eyes tells me she's unhappy. I mean, she's so cold and he looks - well, bored most of the time. I'm guessing he likes the ladies—a lot, so make sure you're on your guard if they invite you around for the evening."

She raises her eyes and whispers, "Keys in the bowl in the centre of the table, if I'm not mistaken."

Now I am definitely not looking at Lucas because I'm guessing he's about to explode—with laughter. Keith says pompously, "Sandra's a good judge of character, she's never wrong."

Looking over at Jasmine and Liam, I see them in a new light. Wow, do things like that really go on outside of the movies? How interesting.

Then Sandra says firmly, "I see you have a cat."

"Yes, Pixie." I smile at the mention of my adored pet and Sandra shakes her head. "Word of warning, make sure you keep it in for a few weeks. Don't let it roam because I'm not going to lie, cats around here are becoming a nuisance."

"In what way?"

I feel a little anxious and Keith says, "Messing over the lawn, sleeping in flowerbeds and on car roofs. Fighting at night and making a terrible noise and generally becoming a right nuisance. I have added it to the agenda at the next committee meeting because something needs to be done about it."

"Yes, take your own cat for instance."

My heart freezes as she says coolly, "I found it in my kitchen this afternoon and had to shoo it away. It comes as something when you can't even leave your door open to air the house without intruders taking up residency. Just so you know, Keith is allergic to animal fur and any trace of it could lead to an anaphylactic shock, so I would ask you to keep your animal under control, otherwise you may have a death on your conscience."

Once again, I open my mouth to speak but Sandra waves at someone gaily from across the kitchen and says loudly,

"Oh, excuse us, I must have a word with Adrian, he told me he would recommend a good landscape gardener and I'm keen to get started."

Keith looks at her proudly. "Yes, Sandra's always been a keen gardener. We opened our last garden to the public under the National Garden scheme. I'm sure she will raise the bar high in the neighbourhood when she gets planning."

As they move away, Lucas growls, "I'll raise the bar myself if I spend one more minute with that woman."

I'm spared from answering as Nancy heads over and raises her eyes, "Sorry to leave you with the Wickhams, please don't judge the rest of us by them."

I instantly relax and laugh softly, "They're an interesting couple, that's for sure."

Giggling, Nancy looks across at her husband and laughs as she sees the pained look he shoots in her direction as Sandra corners him in the kitchen.

Turning to us, she says sweetly, "Let me introduce you to Jasmine and Liam, they are one hundred percent nicer than the Wickhams and the nicest people I know."

We follow her to meet them and I look with interest as we approach.

Jasmine is an attractive woman with long dark hair and stunning blue eyes. She's dressed immaculately and looks to be in her mid-thirties. Her husband looks around him with an easy manner and seems unfazed by his surroundings and comfortable in company and I wonder what he does for a living because they have money, it's obvious by the clothes they wear and the watch on his wrist.

"Jasmine, Liam, meet Esme and Lucas, our new neighbours."

I smile and Lucas steps forward and shakes Liam's hand as Jasmine smiles. "Pleased to meet you. This must be a little overwhelming."

"A little, but it's nice to meet the neighbours."

Liam grins. "Some of them, anyway."

He rolls in eyes in Sandra's direction and I grin.

Jasmine lowers her voice, "You'll soon become de-sensitised to the Wickhams. To be honest, I tuned out five minutes after I met them. They're always moaning about something and if you dare leave your bins out for more than half an hour after the bin men leave, expect a knock on the door and a sharp reprimand from Keith on Sandra's instructions."

Liam laughs. "We do it to annoy them. It's become a favourite game of ours."

Jasmine laughs and looks at him fondly, "One of many, darling."

Lucas nudges me and images of keys in a bowl spring to my mind as the couple share a loaded look.

Turning her attention back to me, Jasmine lowers her voice. "It's not a bad place to live, at least it won't be when they finish it and the builders leave. Most people here seem nice and the Wickham's aside, most appear normal at least."

Liam nods. "You must take Jasmine's word on that, I still think the place is stuffed full of Stepford wives."

He looks at Lucas and nods towards the counter. "Fancy a beer, you could probably use one just to get through this ordeal."

I can sense Lucas's relief as he nods. "Great, now you mention it…"

They move away and I exhale, feeling as if a tremendous weight has lifted and Jasmine laughs. "It's hard for them."

"Who?"

"The men. They suffer at these things because they're like fish out of water. Liam hates mingling with the natives as he calls it and the fact that Lucas seems nice will have helped."

"Why, what about Adrian, he seems nice?"

"He's ok I guess, a little quiet most of the time and not a big drinker. He's content just to follow Nancy around and do what she tells him. He's a bit easily led and doesn't seem to have his own conversation. It's always Nancy this and Nancy that."

"What does he do for a living?"

I look across at the man backed into a corner with interest.

"I think he's an accountant, don't ask me where he works because it left my mind the moment they told me. I'm not going to lie, talk about money bores me rigid, I'm much more interested in hearing the local gossip."

"Then we will get along just fine."

I laugh softly and she grins. "Then let me fill you in."

Steering me to the corner of the window, she points out the houses that back onto ours.

"The house behind this one belongs to a retired couple. I think he's a policeman and they are nice enough. They just keep themselves to themselves and are no trouble. The one next to them, behind you, is a little strange."

"In what way?" The alarm bell rings and Jasmine looks out of the window thoughtfully. "Well, I've been here a while now and still don't know who lives there. The windows are open at the back but there's never anyone in the garden. Occasionally I see a man coming and going and there is a car parked there most nights, but nothing at weekends."

"Maybe they just live there in the week, do you think they have another weekend home somewhere?"

"Possibly, if they do, you're lucky. At least you won't have a child jumping up and down on a trampoline disturbing your peace, or a dog barking while you relax in the garden. In some sense they are the perfect neighbours because they make no sound at all. Maybe I'm wrong, but take a look when you go around to that side. It's the house with the pretty pink door. You can't miss it."

"Are you talking about the house behind Esme's?"

Nancy joins us and says with interest. "I heard it's some kind of company house, you know, the sort companies house their workers in and they go home on weekends. It would explain the state of the garden. I don't think they've weeded since they arrived. You should hear Keith moaning about it, it's quite funny, really."

Jasmine rolls her eyes. "He's only happy if he's moaning. Can you imagine the conversation in that house?"

Nancy laughs. "True enough. Anyway, this is nice, isn't it? Our little quartet is complete and if we can somehow get the Wickhams to move, all would be perfect."

As I look around at the friendly gathering, my heart settles. Yes, this is perfect, to me, anyway and I hope that we will be happy here because I never like to admit I'm wrong and my family's happiness is everything to me. This move is everything to me because I want us to live the life I always wanted us to have, and I've a feeling that Meadow Vale could be just the place to deliver it.

CHAPTER 5

ESME

It doesn't take long to settle into a routine, and one of them is my early morning jog around the development. As soon as I wake, I pull on my running shoes and lycra and start the gentle jog, taking time to admire the place we now call home. As I turn the corner to the village green, my attention is drawn to the house with the pretty pink door. Ever since I heard the gossip about the place, I've been intrigued and have spent many hours just looking out of my window at the house behind us and imagining all sorts.

Jasmine and Nancy were right, they are certainly not keen gardeners because I'm not sure if they've planted one plant since they got there. From what I can see, the lawn is still just an enormous expanse of grass with no flower beds dug out and although it is obviously cut regularly, there is no other sign of life except the windows that are open daily.

As I jog past the front of the property, it's as if nobody's at home. Occasionally, I've seen a black car parked on the driveway, but again no sign of life from the front. The curtains are never open and the windows are dirty, telling me they don't think cleaning them is of any importance. Is it a company house? It could be, and yet for some reason I am developing an unhealthy obsession with the place.

As I jog, I think about our first few weeks here. It didn't take long to settle in and with every passing day; I thank God we moved here. This is the place I've always dreamed of raising my family. Unlike London, the pace of life is slower, the surrounding space bigger, and the air appears cleaner. Gone are the dusty, noisy streets of a city where its inhabitants coexist in close proximity and here in Meadow Vale, the streets are wider, the houses larger and the people friendlier. Well, most of them, anyway.

As I jog around the village green, I look with interest at the houses that back onto ours and see the familiar designs set around a green space with virtually no noise. Maybe it's the lack of life this early in the morning that heightens my senses because for the entire circuit I feel as if I'm being watched. If there were any net curtains here, I would expect to see them twitching because it feels a little eerie as I pass houses impressive in design, hiding their inhabitants behind shuttered windows.

Half way round, my shoelace comes undone and I bend down to tie it, glad of a breather, and as I do, I hear a door slam and look up with interest. A man is heading out of a smart house nearby and as I look up, he raises his hand to wave.

"Good morning."

Straightening up, I smile as he heads my way, briefcase in one hand and his car keys in another.

"Hey, I've seen you most mornings, which leads me to the conclusion you must live here. My name's, Guy and I live here with Angela, my wife. Have you moved here recently?"

Glad of some friendly conversation, I smile, "Pleased to meet you, Guy, yes, I've moved into Sycamore Avenue."

"Welcome, how are you finding it?"

"Good thanks, it's a lovely development, we feel very lucky to live here."

"Yes, same. What house type did you buy?"

"The Rose. We love it."

I look at Guy's house and see a similar house to ours, but a step up in design. It interests me to see the different houses and I'm itching to look inside to see the differences and how they've furnished it.

"Where did you move from?" Guy says with interest and I smile politely. "Streatham."

"This must be quite a change for you then. We moved from Brighton, so it's not a million miles away and was the best thing we ever did."

"You like it here then?" My heart settles as he nods vigorously. "Yes, we should have moved years ago but then again, I'm a firm believer in fate and this place is that for us, anyway. Well, I should get to work. This place costs money and any spare, Angela disposes of extremely quickly. Hopefully we'll see you for drinks one evening. Word of warning, there are a lot of those, maybe it's because everyone's new, we're all keen to establish a community, so don't be surprised if you find yourselves out a lot, it's all good though."

He nods politely. "Well nice to meet you…"

"Esme."

I watch as he heads towards his car and think how nice he seemed. Everyone seems so nice and it strikes me that in the few weeks I've been here, I've met more people than the twenty years I spent in Streatham. We never socialised with our neighbours there. Everyone was too exhausted after working all day and once they closed their front doors, they only opened them for Deliveroo, or to go to work. This is a different life entirely, and I'm keen to see what that involves.

As I start the gentle jog home, I congratulate myself on a

good move made and try to push aside the feeling of uneasiness that won't go away. This is all a little too perfect, a little surreal and as if there's an undercurrent of something that is definitely not normal.

CHAPTER 6

LOLA

The blue sky outside my window tells me it will be another warm day. The birds that wake me are my only company because aside from my nightly visit from Mr Evans, I'm all alone.

As always, as soon as I wake, I drag myself to the window and look out on a place I always knew existed but never thought I'd see first-hand. Smart houses and expensive cars existing in a quiet piece of paradise.

Then, as always, my thoughts turn to my father and the anxiety returns. Where is he, is he ok and when will this be over?

My stomach growls reminding me I haven't eaten in twelve hours and the tears bite at the realisation a visit is due.

When I left with the police officers, I never expected to end up here. They were so nice and made me feel as if I was safe. I am safe, for now, anyway. Is my father ok, it's been a week already and still no word? Mr Evans tells me nothing, just delivers me food and tells me to lie low. I must never be discovered because if I am, it's doubtful I would see my father again.

The air inside the room suffocates me and I struggle to breathe. I am so worried. Is he ok, have they have looked him after like they said he would? Is it over yet and when will I be sent back to him? These are my usual thoughts when I wake and ones that accompany me through the day. It's been several weeks now and still no word.

As I drag myself to the window, I look out at the house opposite eagerly. Are they up yet?

I spend hours at the window, but they will never see me watching. I must stay out of sight; nobody must know I'm here because if I'm discovered they will come for me. I'll never see my father again, so I do as I'm told. 'It won't be long' they say, 'how long?' I ask, but I'm never told a date. The only way I can get through this is to watch the world outside my window carrying on without me.

When the people moved in opposite, I was glad of something new to watch. A normal family. Two small boys and a sweet little cat. Occasionally, I hear their laughter cross the divide towards me and I strain to hear their conversation. I crave the voices because my world is now a silent one. No television, no radio and no communication. I am forbidden to move around the house. In fact, I couldn't if I wanted to because from the moment I arrived, I have been locked in this room with no way out. At least I have a modern bathroom, but nothing else. A single bed and a small table, with only the small bag of possessions I packed and not even a book. I could go mad in here; I feel as if I already am and the only thing left for me to do is watch the world outside my window, remaining hidden because the consequences of being found are too horrific to even think about.

The nightmare never goes away. It's behind my eyes when I sleep at night and sits beside me during the day.

When my father told me what had happened, I was frightened for him. He told me I would be safe and he had arranged a deal with the authorities for my protection. I was to go with the officers to a safe house where I would wait for this to be over.

I'm still waiting.

The days have dragged into weeks and still now word. Mr Evans visits in the evenings but says nothing.

I'm scared of Mr Evans.

He delivers me enough food to see me through to the next visit and says very little. He is gruff and non-communicative and something about the way he looks at me tells me something isn't right. He makes me feel uncomfortable, and yet I'm safe here. It's the deal we made, they are the people sworn to protect us and I will leave soon.

These thoughts are the only ones keeping me going because they've all I've got. Those and my visits from Mr Evans.

A flash of movement draws my attention and I see the curtains open at the house next door to the one opposite. The nice woman is there and my heart beats a little faster as I watch greedily for anything to distract me from the boredom of my life. I like that house - those people. I see them in their garden, laughing and joking. The woman likes to garden. She's there a lot and I've seen her transform it over the weeks with hours spent planting flowers and tidying it up. She has a nice family; I've watched them all. Her husband, at least I think he is, mows the grass and reads his paper in a deck chair facing the sun.

Normal life, I always knew it existed. I watched it on the television and heard tales of it from my friends at school. I never had a normal life. It was always just dad and me. My mum was never around, I can't remember her, anyway. Just me and dad living in a two-bedroom flat in Leicester until the day it all changed and we moved to Brighton. I wish we never had; it's changed everything.

Sighing, I head to the bathroom and prepare to spend an hour relaxing in a bath and getting ready for another day at the window. It's all I have to do, and I have never been so clean. I lie back and sing little songs under my breath in a whisper because I must make no noise. I make up stories in my head where I am happy and in charge of my life. I recite poetry and conjure up happy memories. I do anything and everything to keep myself sane because I will not let what is happening now break me. I will be strong and brave for my dad because I'm the lucky one. I'm guessing he's not finding things so easy because he has a job to do and it's not a pleasant one. No, I must do as I'm told and wait for this to be over.

∽

ANOTHER DAY PASSES and it feels as if it's been two. Time drags when you have so much of it and each hour seems like three as I wait for my freedom.

As the sun sets on another day spent waiting, I hear the garage door opening and the hum of an engine and my heart sinks. Mr Evans' here.

Quickly, I scoot away from the window and sit on the side of the bed nervously. Will I be lucky tonight? He promised me a book to read, a magazine, anything to stifle the boredom of living inside four walls with no exercise. I pray to God that he's remembered because I am going slightly mad in here.

The dull sound of his tread on the staircase causes my heart to thump. I should be happy to see another human being—I'm not. It's Mr Evans, and I'm never happy to see him. Why couldn't it be the other officer who comes? He was nice, kind and concerned. He was considerate and made me feel comfortable. Not Mr Evans. He never speaks, just issues instructions and leaves. Deposits my food and drink and is gone before I can ask the one question I need an answer to more than the food he brings. When am I going home?

I hear the key in the lock turn and my heart beats a little faster. I watch the handle turn with a morbid fascination and as the door inches open just a little, I hold my breath.

"Lola."

His voice is deep and husky and holds just a hint of menace. Is he the bad cop? In my mind he is, and I just stare at him with a frozen expression and clasp my hands to stop them shaking.

He is carrying a tray of food and something else. My eager eyes zone in on the carrier bag he balances on one arm and I try to make out the outline. Is it a book, something to do? I hope so, and I almost can't contain my curiosity as I wait for him to set the tray on the table against the far wall. The door closes softly behind him and I wonder when I may make it through the other side. It may only be a few more days, maybe he has news I very much want to hear, but I bide my time and wait patiently for him to speak.

He turns and his look causes me to shiver inside. What does that look mean? Something I'm not going to like I suspect, and as he tosses me the bag, I reach for it with an eagerness that doesn't surprise me.

"I brought you a few books to read."

The tears burn as I silently offer a prayer to God, thanking him for mercy. Books - the plural. On the one hand it means I have some escape from this strange world I find myself in, but on the other hand, it tells me my time here is not over yet.

I look up as he runs his fingers through his jet-black hair

and notice a sovereign ring glint as the light catches it from the window.

"Come with me."

I look up in surprise and whisper, "What?"

"You heard me; we have an important job to do."

I stand, but my legs are shaking so hard I wonder if I can walk. He turns and opens the door, expecting me to follow and why wouldn't I? Finally, I get to leave the small room and feast my eyes on a different view.

I follow him along the hallway and to the top of the stairs. I fully expect him to head down them, but he moves past them to another room set off at an angle. My heart thumps as I follow him, wondering what this is? I feel nervous because the look in his eye told me I have every right to be.

For a brief second his hand hovers over the door handle as if he is in two minds whether to open it and then he sighs and says tersely, "Follow me."

CHAPTER 7

LOLA

This room is bigger than mine. The window is cloaked in shade and there is no view. It's dark in here and just a little colder. I shiver from that cold as much as the fear that strikes my heart when I see the huge bed dominating the room. There are no covers, just a mattress covered in a black sheet. The walls are bare, with no pictures or decoration of any kind, and I see a wooden chair set in the corner facing the bed. Beside the chair is a wooden table on top of which appears to be some kind of recording equipment and I feel the fear for real for the very first time. Something's wrong.

Mr Evans flicks a switch and I hear the equipment waking up and filling the room with evil.

He nods towards the bed and says abruptly, "Sit on the edge, we need to make a video for your father."

"My father?" At the mere mention of him, my heart lifts. "Is he ok, is it over?"

"No."

The terror strikes me as I stutter, "He's not ok?"

"Yes - no, what I meant was, he needs to see you're ok before he finishes the job."

"Oh."

I sit for a moment, a thousand questions battling to be heard, and I seize my chance and say quickly, "He is safe though—isn't he?"

"Of course, he's just waiting to leave and wanted to see your face before he goes."

"Why can't I call him, Facetime, wouldn't that be better?"

"No."

His voice is rough and brutal and not quite right. Why can't I see my father? He wants to see me, but why like this? There's something he's not telling me and I need answers.

"Then why the video?"

I surprise myself with my question because Mr Evans scares me and just the sight of him frown in my direction causes my heart to race and the panic to set in. He's holding back, I can feel it.

Sighing, he sits on the chair opposite the bed and says in a bored voice, "This is for your own protection, you know that. A phone signal would alert your father's enemies to your location, and that is why we placed you here. If they knew where you were, you wouldn't be safe. It's why you must stay hidden because the moment they find you, we can't protect you anymore."

"Why not, you're the police, you can lock them up?"

Rolling his eyes, he shuts me down in a second. "Do as I say and you may get through this. Now, I want you to look happy, content and above all, safe. Pretend you are talking to him face to face and assure him that everything is ok. He's finding things tough and needs this to see him through the task ahead. Don't fuck it up because if you do, you'll probably never see him again."

He turns to the camera and I sit shaking with fear. Never see him again. How is that even an option? I never knew this thing he had to do was that dangerous. I mean, I know it's risky but never see him again. What does that mean?

As I face the camera with my ankles crossed and my hands in my lap, I appear calm and collected. Inside is a raging torrent of emotions that's hard to navigate. Can I pull this off, it's becoming increasingly obvious I need to because my father's life depends on him seeing that I'm ok? So, as Mr Evans gives me the thumbs up, I do what is necessary to keep my father safe.

Smiling into the camera, I say lightly,

"I miss you dad. A tear tries to find an escape route, but I blink it hastily away and try to smile when inside my heart is breaking.

"I just want you to know I'm fine, they are looking after me well and I'm just counting down the days until we're back together. I have a warm bed and food and some books to occupy my time. I hope you have everything you want too and are thinking of me as much as I'm thinking about you. The place I'm staying in is nice and the people friendly."

I pray that the guilt doesn't betray me because I feel hot under the collar as I blatantly lie to my father. Whatever happens, I have it easier than him and he needs to think everything is ok.

It's strange sitting in a bedroom with Mr Evans watching, talking to a camera, but I imagine my father on the other side of it desperately looking to see if I'm ok. I fix a smile on my face and make my voice light and care free. I want him to feel good about this call because I'm guessing he's struggling just as much as I am and needs his mind put to rest. So, I babble on about how amazing this place is and talk about the people I've seen through the window as if they are actually friends of mine. I suppose I get so carried away in my descriptions, I forget that my every move is being watched by a pair of unfriendly eyes. It's only as the conversation falters that I see Mr Evans throwing me a look that makes me feel uncomfortable.

As I say goodbye to my father, assuring him we will soon be reunited, I realise something is definitely wrong.

With another flick of the wrist, the equipment stops and there is just silence laced with an uneasy sense of foreboding. My heart pounds as Mr Evans looks at me a little differently and I shiver inside.

Then he says roughly, "I told you to stay hidden. From your conversation it's obvious you've been spending rather a long time at that window and it's only a matter of time before someone sees you, if they haven't already."

I'm not sure why, call it self-preservation, but I shake my head and blurt, "I made them up."

His eyes narrow and he leans forward as if looking into the deep recesses of my mind. "You. Made. Them. Up."

He savours every word as if it starts a new sentence, and the hairs on the back of my neck stand to attention.

Don't ask me why, but what happens next is very important to me and I remain impassive and shrug. "There's nothing else to do."

He stares at me a little harder as if willing me to break and confess everything, but somehow, I feel as if I've dodged a bullet when he growls, "Back to your room."

I shift off the bed and almost run to the door because this room unnerves me. There's a sense of something not right here, and yet I don't know what.

I head back and as I pass the staircase, look down them longingly at the front door, welcoming me through it like a beacon of safety. Why do I feel unsafe in what should surely be a safe house? Because of him. The way he looks at me and the promise of something out of my control lurking behind the corner.

As he follows me out of the room, I say impulsively, "I want to go downstairs."

I'm surprised when he grabs my arm and forces me towards the door of my room, growling, "I don't give a fuck what you want. This is for your own protection and you don't have options. Just be grateful your cell is so luxurious because we can arrange a different holding tank for you if you don't cooperate."

He almost throws me inside the room and says harshly, "Stay away from the window, or else."

He slams the door leaving me reeling. Or else what?

I hear the key turn in the lock and stand in the middle of the room wondering what the hell just happened. This isn't right, surely.

I wander over to the table and note the food laid out for me. A bottle of water, a pack of sandwiches, a salad and some fruit. A packet of biscuits and a flask of tea. Hardly enough to keep me going through a few hours, let alone twelve. I know he'll be back tomorrow, early in the morning before the neighbour's wake. That meal will see me through to the evening and once again I will anticipate his visit with excitement because it's the only thing that happens during my day.

However, this time it's different because I see the innocent looking carrier bag holding some welcome entertainment. Books.

Quickly, I hurry over and empty the contents onto the bed and see two books gleaming up at me.

Reaching for the first one, I see a classic, Jane Austen, Pride and Prejudice. Not my usual choice, but beggars can't be choosers. Then I turn my attention to the other one and see a pretty cottage on the front, set by the sea. A light romance, something to lighten the darkness and make me believe in happy endings.

Seizing the book like a lifeline, I savour the moment. I turn the pages and see the words dancing like light before my eyes, and I sink down onto the bed and set about escaping my situation for as long as possible.

CHAPTER 8

ESME

Jasmine's house is bigger than ours and her furniture more modern. I can't stop staring as I walk through her hallway into her brightly lit kitchen and compare her house to mine.

"You have a lovely home, Jasmine, how long have you been here now?"

"Six months."

"You'd never know it, it's very stylish, almost a show home."

Jasmine laughs softly and flicks the kettle on. "It should resemble one because we used the same company who did the show home on the development. It was just easier to get them to do it for us, and then all we had to do was unpack our suitcases."

"Didn't you have any furniture then?" I stare at her in shock because who has no furniture, but she just shrugs and turns away, mumbling, "We just thought we'd start afresh."

I can tell she doesn't want to elaborate, so I just shrug and take a seat at the counter on a bar stool, feeling jealous of the calm interior, free from clutter and crap, as Lucas calls our stuff.

I try to beat down my jealousy as she whips up a coffee from an impressive-looking machine and bite down the envy as she shakes some expensive cookies onto a plate, before reaching across and pulling a cake stand towards us containing a mouth-watering walnut and coffee cake under a sparkling glass dome.

"Did you make this?"

I stare at the impressive creation in awe as she nods. "Yes, I found the recipe online. I can give it to you if you like."

"Great, I'd love that, thanks."

Feeling very inadequate, I take the plate she pushes my way and spear the small pastry fork into the mouth-watering cake and savour the taste of something I could never recreate given all the cookery lessons in the world.

As she joins me, I note how tired she looks and wonder if she's been working until the early hours again. I often see a light on in her study when I head to bed at midnight and see her crouched over the computer with the desk lamp illuminating her concentration.

She runs her fingers through her hair and smiles wearily. "Sorry, I've been working on a case all night and should really have got some sleep."

Immediately I feel guilty and say quickly, "You should have cancelled, I would understand."

"No, of course I wouldn't." She waves my comment away and raises her black coffee to her painted red lips and sighs. "It goes like this sometimes. It's all or nothing with my job, and there are never enough hours in the day. Other times I can relax and enjoy my days without feeling the pressure of a deadline."

"What are you working on, can I ask, or is it top secret?"

I am fascinated by this woman, her life, her job - *her husband.*

That thought shocks me as I glance at the framed silver photo on the wall by the dining table and see them staring out at me. His arm is slung around her shoulder and their heads are together as they smile for the camera. They look so happy and carefree, and I wonder what their story is?

Jasmine sighs and runs her fingers through her long shiny black hair. "It's a hard case involving child porn. I hate these more than anything because it's impossible to remain impartial. I want to castrate the bastard with a rusty knife but I have to defend him and make excuses for him; try to find a loop hole to set the monster free and it hurts my soul to do it."

I stare at her in horror and whisper, "Can't you hand it over to someone else, this is awful?"

"Not really, we have to earn the right to pick our cases and I have a lot to prove. You see, I operate in a man's world and it's hard to catch a break. I have to be smarter, more resilient and a ball-breaker to stand any chance and sometimes it's tempting to chuck the lot in and bake cakes at home and hang the money."

"Why don't you find another company, or set up on your own?"

She stares at me as if I'm an idiot and I probably am because I know nothing about her life and then she sighs. "Maybe I will but for now, I have to put up and shut up because we have stretched ourselves to the max to buy this place and no matter how difficult it is, I must do my bit."

She looks at me with interest. "So, how are you finding life in Meadow Vale? Is it how you imagined it, or are the dark shadows claiming your soul already?"

I look up in surprise and she grins wickedly. "You're

wondering what I'm talking about, well, let me enlighten you."

Suddenly I'm all ears as she leans forward and whispers, "Behind every door here is a story to tell. Respectability dressing up depravity."

Now I'm all ears, as I whisper, "What do you mean?"

"Well, I've told you about the house with the pretty pink door. I mean, who really knows what goes on there, but it's the others you should really worry about?"

"Others?"

I feel slightly nervous as she laughs darkly. "Keith and Sandra hide it well, but I've seen the cameras."

"Cameras?"

I feel faint as she smirks. "Trained all over the place, it's like MI5 in their study. I popped round there once to return one of Keith's endless questionnaires and saw a bank of monitors set up with our houses in the starring role."

"They're spying on us?"

"You bet they are."

"But isn't that illegal?"

"Yes, but he dresses it up as security and protection against thieves and vandals. There's a reason he likes to run the committee on this place. You mark my words. Who knows what else he has his camera lens trained on?"

Suddenly, she laughs and a wicked glint sparks in her eye. "Take Nancy and Adrian, for example, it's not all 2.5 children and mowing the lawn on Sundays there."

"Really."

I lean forward again and feel my heart beating with excitement. Jasmine is amazing and I can't get enough of her conversation.

"Word is, Nancy's son was expelled from his last school for filming the girls in the changing room."

"Who told you that?"

"Sandra Wickham, of course. I mean, he's nice enough but spends a lot of time playing on his computer and he has one of those drones that he often flies around the place."

"Isn't that illegal?"

"Yes, but he says it's just a hobby and there's no recording equipment in it. Well, what he says and what he does are two very different things."

Her laughter cracks the tension in the room and she says brightly, "Yes, this is your typical housing development, respectable on the outside but when those front doors close, they hide a multitude of sins. What I want to know, though, is what hides behind yours?"

My face must betray my shock because she laughs and raises a forkful of cake to her lips. "Don't mind me, Esme, I spend so long wallowing in filth, I kind of expect it. Pay no attention to my stories because that's all they are—stories. I'm sure there are perfectly innocent explanations for everything you see around here, and it's only my overactive imagination that corrupts them into something much more interesting."

The doorbell interrupts us, and I'm almost grateful for a moment alone to process what she's told me. Surely this is a safe place. She must be wrong because everyone seems nice and can't possibly be the type of people she describes.

I look up as Nancy enters, carrying a wicker basket with the most mouth-watering smell emanating from it.

"Sorry I'm late but I had to wait for the brownies to cool. Adrian's also hanging some wallpaper in the spare bedroom and needed me to hold the ladder." She rolls her eyes and says painfully, "I need the strongest coffee you've got because he's no decorator. I swear he matched the pattern all wrong and yet as soon as I mentioned it, he went into one of his sulks. Men. I wish they would just knock on the door when needed. It would be a lot easier than dealing with tantrums and arguments 24/7."

She places the basket on the counter and I feel bad that I brought nothing with me. Making a mental note, I vow to dust off my Mary Berry cookbook and return the favour very soon.

For a while, I just listen to the conversation as they chat about how things work around here and people that I've yet to meet. It's very interesting hearing it but I'm left feeling more inadequate than I was when I first sat down. I don't belong here—*we* don't belong here because as hard as I try, I will never be one of them because I just don't have the foggiest idea where to start.

CHAPTER 9

ESME

As soon as I get home, I'm like a demented Martha Stewart. Nothing is safe as I thoroughly de-clutter and spring clean our house, striving for show house perfection. Deciding to become a culinary goddess on another day, I hope the takeaway options are good around here because I have no time for cookery while the house is a mess. Armed with bin bags, I blow through the house like a tornado and sweep surfaces and try to bring my house into shape. Nothing is safe as I strive for perfection and make it my mission to drag my family up to meet the expectations living here demands.

As I drag my rubbish to the wheelie bins around the side of the house, I look up at the property opposite and wonder what secrets it hides. As usual, the window on the top floor is open and yet there is no other sign of life. I squint in the sunshine as I look for any movement or reflection, but see nothing.

I wonder if Jasmine is just messing with my mind because I can't imagine there is anything strange going on around here. I mean, everyone seems so nice and, well, normal.

"What's going on?"

I head inside and see Lucas looking at me as if I've gone mad.

"What do you mean?"

"This place, where is everything?"

"If you're referring to the general clutter, you will find it in the bin. We no longer need it in our lives, and I can't believe we brought so much with us."

"Are you mad?"

Lucas storms past me and starts rifling through the bin, throwing objects to the ground and moaning, "For god's sake, Esme, this isn't your stuff to throw. I need these things. What else have you interfered with?"

"Nothing, I've just got started but things are about to change, Lucas. We need to shape up because we're living like pigs. Look at this place, it's a brand-new house and we have filled it with rubbish. I want us to start again and look as if we belong here."

"Are you serious, what do you mean, look as if we belong here, are you insane?"

"No, just bringing our family to the level we should be. There's no harm in trying to better yourselves, and this is the perfect place to start."

I try not to see the distaste on Lucas's face as I study him with a critical eye. Slightly scruffy, wearing his usual jeans and t-shirt, not to mention the tattoos that I always knew would be a bad idea. No, it's time to shape up and I vow to start with him and style him exactly the same as… Something stops me as I contemplate what I just thought. Do I really want Lucas to be exactly like Liam? What's happening to me? Five minutes here and I'm doubting my choice in life in favour of something I think I want.

Lucas just looks at me angrily and storms off with all his

rubbish and I shake the disturbing thoughts away and shout after him, "Make sure you put that stuff where I can't see it."

The slamming door is my answer and I look up at the house facing ours in dismay. I hope nobody picked up on Lucas's petty tantrum. Goodness, whatever will the neighbour's think?

∽

BY THE TIME the boys come home from school, I have removed every cardboard box from their rooms and put all their belongings away into the cupboard. The house is looking better, there is less clutter, and I've even placed a tablecloth on our ring-marked wooden table to hide the evidence.

The boys look at me in surprise as I smile with what I believe a loving mother looks like and say pleasantly, "How was your day my darlings?"

Archie just looks at his brother and shrugs, and Billy mutters under his breath, "Weird."

They turn to wrench open the fridge door and grab armfuls of food before I shriek, "Stop right there. Put the food back and walk away, immediately. Straight to your rooms and change out of your uniforms. I'll make you a healthy snack while you do your homework."

They just stare at me as if I've grown two heads and I say sharply, "Now, if you value your leisure time this evening."

"What's going on?"

Archie looks confused and I say firmly, "Beginning today, we will behave like a normal family. This is the new normal and if you know what's best for you, you'll adopt it with no arguments. Now scoot and do as I say, otherwise there will be no healthy snacks for you to enjoy."

They just look at each other and Billy shrugs and heads upstairs to his room, closely followed by his brother.

Feeling some sense of victory, I turn and open the fridge in pursuit of a healthy snack to honour my promise and my heart sinks. There isn't one.

Chocolate, cold sausages, some milk past its best and a mouldy piece of brie. Where are the healthy homemade, lovingly prepared, muesli bars that would look good next to a fruit smoothie? Come to think of it, where is the fruit in this place because frankly my fridge is a disgrace?

Sighing, I reach for the biscuit tin and lay out two rich tea biscuits each and pour them a glass of water, resolving to fix this first thing tomorrow morning by doing a large shop.

Lucas heads back and rolls his eyes. "What's got into you, the boys think you've been abducted by aliens? You know, Esme, if I thought moving here would make you into a snob, I would never have agreed. This isn't you - us. Stop trying to be something you're not."

I feel the anger bubbling up and snap, "How do you know I'm not? Maybe I've always wanted to be more than the woman I became. Perhaps I want to better us as a family and make us reach our full potential. There's nothing wrong with that, Lucas, just think about it and you'll know I'm talking sense."

"What's for tea?" He shrugs off my comments as if they're not worth considering and I seethe inwardly and say pompously, "Supper tonight is chicken carbonara with garlic bread."

He groans and I turn my back on him. One step at a time because my offering tonight will be the last ready meal I buy. From now on I will beat these women at their own game and become some sort of perfect housewife, wife and mother and I'm going to do it while I look for part time work to pay for it all.

. . .

LATER THAT NIGHT as I close the curtains, something makes me look across at the house behind us. The shutters are closed as usual and the window open. The house is always in darkness, I expect that, but tonight something is different. Tonight, one shutter hasn't been closed properly and I can see a small sliver of light shining through the slats. I don't turn away and just look a little harder, but I can't see a thing, just the light. Somebody's there, it's obvious. I wonder who they are, and maybe I should try and find out. We are neighbours, after all, and I know just what excuse I will use when I go round there.

CHAPTER 10

JASMINE

"Babe, where are my glasses?"

"Where they always are, on the side in your study."

I turn back and stare at the computer screen, feeling the bile rise in my throat. Vincent Debruges stares back at me with the cold eyes of a sexual predator. He gives me the creeps and I feel physically sick every time I meet him. I begged my boss to find someone else, but he was adamant it had to be me. I'm not stupid, I know he's had it in for me since I arrived. Word is, he wanted the position filled by his buddy from university but the powers that be wanted a woman to balance their diversity levels. It's no wonder I have to work extra hard to gain any approval from the men I work with because they just look at me as a ticked box – a statistic that prevents their company from adverse publicity at a later date.

Sighing, I try to study the case as if my eyes are a microscope looking for ways to plead his case. It's obvious he's guilty, from the evidence taken from the victims and the video evidence from the children involved. Two of the children were from his own family and the hurt and betrayal in the eyes of them and both parents will live with me to my dying day. I hope I lose this case and the bastard gets three life sentences and never gets out. I hope this man pays the price in an extremely violent way in prison and I hope he suffers because what he did to those poor children will affect them and everyone who knows about it to their dying day.

The door opens softly and Liam moves behind me and I relax as the familiar scent of whisky and tobacco fills my senses. "Come to bed."

I lean back as he massages my shoulders and his breath fans my neck as he gently nips at the side causing me to melt. If I had one wish right now, it would be to do exactly as he says, but I don't have that luxury because this case is too important to let slide, so I say with bitterness, "You know I can't."

He increases the pressure and I moan gently as he runs his fingers under my top and strokes my skin like a favourite pet. He spins the office chair to face him and drops to his knees, taking my lips in his and demanding entrance. Clasping my head, he punishes me with his tongue, tying mine with his and demonstrating that 'no' is not an option. It never was when it came to him, which is why we're here today.

He pushes my skirt up with his other hand and gently traces a path to my thigh and as if by magic, my legs fall apart as easily as they always have – for him.

Yes, I can deny Liam Davis nothing and never could, and even the thought of failure makes no difference at all as I allow him to pull me from my chair and against his hard body.

As Liam gets what he wants as always, Vincent De Bruges

stares out from the computer screen, a silent reminder that my life's not perfect and probably never will be.

~

No amount of coffee will keep me awake and with a sinking feeling, I slip one of my pills into my mouth and take a sip of cool water from the fridge. I worked until 3am and it's now 5. Two hours of a fitful sleep before I leave for London and another day spent trying to build a guilty man into an innocent one. Liam is still sleeping and I wonder how he does it. Nothing fazes him, he just carries on regardless and always seems to land on his feet. A quick shag in my office was as much attention as I could give him yesterday and I know his patience will soon run thin. Liam is, and always was, an extremely sexual man and likes it regularly and won't take a simple 'no' for an answer.

Briefly, I watch him sleep and my heart settles. It was worth it; it was all worth it because of him - this house and our new life. Once this case is over, I will book us a much-needed holiday and indulge in two glorious weeks with the man I love. They owe me the time off and Liam never has to worry about that as he is the boss of the building company he owns on the outskirts of Brighton. Business is good and money is no object, time though is scarce and I vow to make a little more of it for him because if I don't, I'm under no illusions I could lose him.

As soon as I'm showered, dressed and fed, I grab my briefcase and laptop and head outside. Flicking the electronic device to my BMW, I climb into the sports car and shiver slightly as my bare legs hit the leather surface of the seats. The mornings are crisp and cold and yet it's still summer and as the sun warms the air as the day goes on, the last thing I need is warm clothing to make me uncomfortable.

The sun is rising majestically in the sky, bathing the dawn in a rosy glow, and I take a moment to snap the pink sky that proves what a miracle worker Nature is. Nothing can compare to her mastery, and I love that I get to see her at her best before the day takes over.

All around the development, the inhabitants sleep and the shuttered windows hide their occupants behind them. I always envy them their safe, warm beds as I start the commute to my office in London.

Life would be so much easier if I worked from home, or not at all, as is the case for most of the women here. Marriage and babies, the perfect home and a loving husband, how I used to turn my nose up at that, now I realise its power because as it turns out, I want nothing more.

As I back out from the driveway, my heart sinks as I realise that when I return the sun will be setting. It will be a different photograph I take and one that shows I've missed out on another day spent in suburbia, living the life I always dreamt of. However, that will have to be put on hold until I am established in a company many would kill to work at. Hammers and Goldstein, a law firm in the prestigious Canary Wharf and well known in its field. I am one of several solicitors working on this case and today we have a meeting with Geoffrey Monroe, the Barrister in charge of defending our despicable client.

Geoffrey Monroe is very good at his job and any information we feed him better be factual and researched impeccably because he will strip it bare and call out any mistakes before morning coffee.

I can't be the person who fails in that roomful of men, all waiting for the inevitable to happen. I know they will scrutinise my work more closely and reserve their harshest criticism for whatever I present. It's always been the same and I can't see it changing in the foreseeable future, but I am determined to make it. I'll show them and I'll show them well.

As I make my way to the end of our little street, I stop at the junction to check the road is clear. It always is because nobody else leaves at 5.30am every day, but today I must wait because a black car is crawling towards me and I look with interest. I know that car.

For a moment, I just watch as it passes me and turns into the driveway of the house with the pretty pink door. I hesitate as the lights dim and the door opens and I lift my phone to pretend I'm texting, buying me a little more time to observe. I've never seen the person who lives here and I'm mildly curious, so as a leg swings from the door onto the driveway, I shift my car in gear and crawl past, winding the window down and smiling brightly at the man who looks at me in surprise.

"Hi, I don't think we've met."

I stop at the end of his driveway and he looks up in surprise as he hears me speak.

He looks confused and I wave my hand towards Sycamore avenue. "I live around the corner, we're neighbours of sorts, it's good to meet you."

He nods and appears a little unsure what to do next, so I say in a friendly voice, "I'm Jasmine, sorry I didn't catch your name."

I can tell he feels uncomfortable, but he's backed into a corner, so he shuffles towards my car and says politely, "Charlie."

"I'm pleased to meet you, Charlie, sorry to accost you on your doorstep but it appears we are the only ones who work unsociable hours in this place. Do you work nights, I hope I'm not keeping you from your bed?"

"Sometimes, not always."

"Ah, shift work, what is it you do?"

He appears irritated but that's never bothered me before, many people are irritated by my questions and I ask them, anyway. It's a thirst for knowledge I've always had along with a suspicious mind and from where I'm sitting, this man has 'suspicious' written all over him."

"Security."

He smiles and says quickly, "Sorry, it's been a long night, it was nice to meet you… um… Jasmine."

"Same, oh, and Charlie…"

He stops and I almost see him sigh as he says wearily, "Yes?"

"You must come over for drinks one evening and meet the rest of the neighbours. Shall I drop an invitation into your wife later?"

I can tell he's not happy as he looks exasperated and snaps, "I'm not married."

He runs his fingers through his hair as if the answer to his problems lie there and then sighs and heads toward me, leaning down and mumbling, "To be honest, I'm a bit of a loner. I like to keep myself to myself and don't really have the time for social events. Thanks for the offer though, but I must say no. Now, if you'll excuse me."

He turns away and this time I watch him go, saying nothing until the door clicks shut behind him.

As I start the engine and close the window, I think about what I discovered. Charlie, whatever his name is, was lying through that grim cruel mouth of his because I know how to spot a lie a mile away. Firstly, he was wearing a wedding ring and yet said he wasn't married. Maybe he's divorced or separated. That could be the case. Then the look in his eyes when I asked what he did was the one I see most days when the guilty try to think of something quickly to disguise reality. Whatever his job is, it's not security because I know what I saw and I see it every day. A guilty man thinking on his feet to escape the truth. However, there was something familiar about his face that made me sit up and take notice. I know that face, but I can't think where from. Who is Charlie from the house with the pretty pink door because if he's in security, I'm tucked up safely in bed?

CHAPTER 11

LOLA

He's back. The door slamming wakes me and I'm immediately awake. Mr Evans rarely slams the door; he moves like a thief in the night most days, but the thump of his heavy boots on the stairs warns me that something is different today. Maybe it's not him. Perhaps it's the nice cop this time. I hope so because I haven't seen him since they drove me here in the early hours of the morning what must be three weeks ago.

I almost don't have time to grab my cardigan to wrap around my shaking shoulders before the door opens and he heads inside, cursing under his breath, "Bloody woman, fucking busybody."

I say nothing as he slams a box of supplies on the table and turns and looks at me with a cool expression.

Maybe it's my imagination, but something's different about the way he looks at me today. Perhaps I'm still asleep because I detect a shift in the atmosphere as he leans against the wall and stares at me with an inscrutable expression. It makes me feel uncomfortable and I grasp the cardigan a little tighter around my shoulders as he pushes off from the wall and comes and sits beside me on the bed.

My mouth dries as he raises his hand and touches my face and my breathing intensifies as I see interest spark in his eyes that wasn't there before. "How old are you?"

My heart races as I say nervously, "Fifteen."

His touch feels unwelcome, hot and dangerous, and I shift slightly back. If I thought that was all it would take to stop whatever this is, I was mistaken as he says roughly, "Have you ever been with a man?"

The danger in the room is palpable and I blink the tears away as I whisper, "No."

He leans in and his breathing has changed, it's faster, deeper and all I can hear, as he grasps the back of my head and pulls me towards him until our lips almost touch.

I'm not sure what to do and wonder if I should just close my eyes and pretend he isn't here because this is frightening me—*he is* frightening me because I know something changed the minute he looked at me.

With a low growl, he presses his lips to mine and kisses me brutally, hard and the feeling of his tongue in my mouth makes me want to gag.

I push him away but that only makes him increase his pressure and with a soft laugh he growls, "Do you think you can stop me?"

I am so terrified I don't know what to do and try to pull away, but it only serves to excite him more. He pulls back and grips my throat with his strong fingers and presses me back onto the bed, cutting off my air supply and causing me to panic. He lifts my t-shirt and his fingers find my breasts and he twists one painfully and then says darkly, "I wonder what your daddy would say if he saw you now? Maybe I should show him what happens when he pisses me off."

His fingers press against my throat and I almost think my

time on earth is up until he releases me and I gasp for air. Then before I know what's happening, he rips my t-shirt in half, exposing my body and says harshly, "Open your legs."

The panic sets in as he laughs cruelly and using his knee pushes my legs apart until I'm bare before him. Then he takes his phone and snaps a picture of me and laughs softly, "Maybe I'll frame this and give it to him as a souvenir of the time he pissed me right off."

The bed sags as he moves off and heads toward the door, and my heart beats so fast, I wonder if I'm about to die from fright. The mention of my father replaced my fear of this situation with a fear for him. The way Mr Evans spoke about him was frightening because something's happened. Something that has angered him, and I wonder what that means. What has daddy done?

As the door slams behind him he turns the key and I hear him say, "I'll look forward to seeing you later Lola, I'll have more time to spend with you then. Make sure you're ready for me."

His laughter is the last thing I hear as I stare at the locked door in shock. What just happened, it's all changed now? I'm not safe because Mr Evans has shown me the side to him I always suspected was there and there is nothing I can do about it.

∼

THE NEXT FEW hours are the most worrying of my life. I spent so long in the shower scrubbing my body, trying to remove the imprint of his hands on me, but it doesn't work. It's as if he branded me and I can still see the angry bruising on my throat developing, as a reminder of what he can do. I'm at his mercy here and there is no way out. I consider opening the window and jumping out, but I'm so high up here I would break my neck. Then again, I would have to smash the glass because there is some kind of limiter applied to it that means it only opens so far before it stops. The shutters are locked in place and I can only open them a little and I feel so frustrated I could cry.

I'm trapped.

I look out and see the woman opposite hanging out her washing and I will her to look in my direction. To somehow see me, desperate and in need of her help, but she doesn't even look my way once. Maybe if I pounded on the window, she would hear me and I consider doing just that because I am so frightened right now.

Pressing my lips to the crack in the window, I contemplate calling for help and then an image of the desperation in my father's eyes stops me. If I do this, if I escape, or draw attention to myself, he will suffer. People would know I was here and his enemies would come for me.

My mind drifts back to the night I arrived here and the friendly cop sat beside me on the bed and looked at me with compassion. I remember the conversation as if it just happened.

"You must be scared, Lola, but you're safe here. This is what we call a safe house, and it's called that for a reason. This will be your home for a few weeks while your father does what he must, to resolve the situation he's in. He's upset some corrupt men and its up to us to help him put them behind bars, so they can never hurt anyone again."

"What did he do?"

I feel so frightened because the thought of my father in trouble makes me weak with fear and the nice cop smiles reassuringly and says softly, "We need him to testify against them. He saw something that means they can't escape justice this time. The trial is scheduled a few weeks from now, but until that happens you aren't safe. We have assured him we will keep you safe until it's over and they are behind bars in return for his help."

"Why can't he stay here with me?"

"Because we need him at the station. He will spend the next few weeks helping us sew this case up so there are no cracks for the criminals to escape justice through. These men are desperate and cruel, and if they discover where you are, they will use you to get to him. They may even kill you and we won't let that happen. So, I can't stress this enough. You must stay out of sight because if they find you, they will kill you and it won't be quick."

I remember the fear, the panic and the desperation I felt for a situation totally out of my control. The only thing I could do to help was to do as I was told. Remain here in this room, out of sight and waiting for it all to be over but now… What has daddy done to antagonise Mr Evans so much? What just happened was wrong, I know it was, no cop would do that unless he was corrupt. Maybe he isn't who he said he was, but he must be. I saw their warrant cards; I saw proof they were detectives. My dad said they were and he wouldn't lie. But Mr Evans, he's so scary and appears on edge. Is this a safe house, or the pit of Hell because far from feeling protected here, I just feel the air laced with threat and tension and the promise that when—if I ever leave here, I will leave a very different person than I was when I arrived.

CHAPTER 12

JASMINE

It's been a hard day and one I want to forget and it gets even worse when I pull up on my driveway as the dusk chases the sunshine away and Sandra Wickham calls out, "May I have a word, Jasmine?"

Gritting my teeth, I plaster a smile on my face and say brightly, "Sandra, how are you today?"

She looks at me with a brief nod and cuts to the chase, sweeping aside any pleasantries as if she has no time for them. "I just wanted to mention the state of your front garden. I'm sorry, but those weeds need dealing with. They affect our grass because the wind blows their seeds on to our newly seeded lawn and I'm not prepared to let weeks of care and concentration be destroyed by your neglect."

Her stare warns me against any arguments because she's right. Liam and I aren't gardeners and don't bother trying to be. Compared to her immaculate Stepford garden, ours is a wilderness. I suppose she has every right to complain, so I smile sweetly and nod. "Of course, I'll see to it in the morning."

"Mm, make sure you do because high winds are predicted

over the next few days and the damage may have been done already."

I turn to leave and she shouts, "Oh, and another thing."

My heart sinks. "I wanted to arrange a gathering to welcome our new neighbours. Shall we say 7 o'clock on Friday evening? Just an intimate gathering of the four of us being the first ones here and in our role of committee members, we should be the ones to host the event."

In my mind I count to ten because even the sound of her voice irritates me. It's like a thousand darts piercing my skin in rapid succession, and it takes all my self-control to remain pleasant. "I thought Nancy's party did that, they've already met us all."

"Oh, that."

She waves her hand dismissively and sneers, "That was just for starters. No, I'm talking of the main event. Really getting to know them and laying down a few ground rules. I mean, it's imperative we find out the sort of people they are. For starters, they have two unruly little boys and a feral animal. They need reminding that we live in a respectable neighbourhood and have standards that must be met. I expect no less than they sign up to be active members of the neighbourhood watch committee because numbers are scarce and it shouldn't be up to the minority to protect the masses, don't you agree, Jasmine?"

I shrink under her sharp gaze because I have resisted every one of her attempts to draw me into her tedious committee and so I just shrug. "If they have the time, sure, why not? Mind you, I'm sure their time would be better spent keeping their family and pet under control because god forbid, we would actually enjoy some life in this place. Now, if you'll excuse me, I've had an extremely trying day and need a large gin to make me forget about it."

Sandra Wickham narrows her eyes and the look she

shoots me could extract a person's soul. Her lips are thin and disapproving as she says tightly, "Hmm, I can see that you need something to settle your mood, that's for sure. Now, remember the garden and shall we say Friday 7pm? If you don't mind, please can you bring a tray of canapes as your contribution, along with a bottle of red. Oh, and Jasmine..."

"Yes." I resist the urge to roll my eyes as she says firmly, "The weeds—remember?"

"Of course, consider it done."

Turning my back on her, I put the key in the lock and relish the sound of it shutting the world outside. Silence, pure delicious silence, and I feel as if I can finally breathe again. I never thought this day would end and finding Sandra Wickham waiting for me, was the icing on the cake. Vile woman! I wish I could have vetted the neighbours before we moved in. I'm not sure anyone would want to buy a house next to the Wickhams. Maybe that's why they lived in an enormous mansion with no neighbours for many years. I've lost count of the times she's told me how they made the tough decision to downsize from their gated property in Surrey to a more manageable home. They have a lot to learn about getting along with people because from where I'm standing, they are failing miserably.

Liam is waiting in the kitchen, sitting in his usual place watching the television, drink in hand, and I smile as I catch his eye. "Thank god, a normal person, I missed you."

"Bad day?"

"You could say that."

He pats the seat beside him and winks. "Come over here and let me make it all better."

Kicking off my shoes, I need no further invitation and curl up beside him on the settee and love the way his arm automatically wraps around me and pulls me close. I note the large whisky he has poured himself and frown.

"What's up?"

Liam likes his drinks neat and appears to have half a large glass of his favoured tipple and he sighs heavily. "I spoke to my mum today."

Immediately, I tense up and am fearful to ask but say nervously, "And…?"

"Still not good."

"Oh."

I squeeze my eyes tightly shut and wish like crazy things were different.

He strokes my shoulder absentmindedly and I hate the break in his voice as he sighs, "I don't know what to do about it."

"I know."

Thinking about Liam's mum, Virginia Davis, my heart breaks all over again. I've always loved her and looked on her as a friend more than anything—a best friend who I adored spending time with. Not anymore. Not since Liam and I shattered our perfect lives and those of everyone around us."

I watch as he sets the glass down and pulls me around to face him. My breath hitches as I see the pain in his expression and the shadows that will probably never go away.

He strokes the side of my face and whispers, "It changes nothing."

"Are you sure about that?"

My voice sounds weak and fearful, mirroring what I feel inside, and he smiles reassuringly. "We've come too far already. Time will heal us; we just have to be patient."

"Are you sure we have that - time, I mean."

"We can only hope, not expect. If things never change, we have to live with that. We knew it would be like this , but we went there, anyway. No regrets, Jasmine, you know we have to stay strong."

He kisses me softly and my heart settles. He's right. We

must stay strong and see this through. There must be no backing down and no regretting our decision. It was made for a very good reason—love and what is better than that.

CHAPTER 13

JASMINE

Esme and Lucas seem nice enough. I watch them with interest as they move around the group, both on their best behaviour, as we all are really. The fact we are all new means we are keen to establish friendships and Liam and I could use all the friends we can get at the moment, so I keep a smile on my face and appear interested even when I'm dying inside, which is usually the case when I talk to the Wickham's.

As expected, Sandra has pulled out all the stops and provided an evening that the rest of us would struggle to reciprocate. Having the larger house on our street, she reminds us of that every other sentence and I struggle not to roll my eyes when I hear her say to Esme, "Yes, of course your house is much smaller than ours, I keep on forgetting."

Catching Lucas's eye, I grin as he raises his eyes and excuses himself, leaving his wife to shoulder the Wickham responsibility on her own.

As he heads our way, Liam offers him a beer. "Here you go, you'll need a few of these to get through this evening."

Lucas pulls a face and says in a low voice, "Thanks, I think that woman just got hold of my last nerve and jumped on it. Honestly, I'm not sure how much more of this I can take."

Liam nods. "You'll get used to it. Luckily, we manage to avoid them most of the time, but occasionally you have to take one for the team."

Spotting Nancy looking a little lost, I make my way over to her and she smiles with relief when she sees me coming.

"Thank God, a normal conversation at last. I've just spent twenty minutes discussing planning applications and snagging lists with Keith. I'm sorry, Jasmine, but there's only so much I can take."

"Tell me about it. I spent all morning weeding just so they didn't find their way into their Chelsea inspired front garden."

"Maybe you should build a wall."

We laugh and Nancy whispers, "What do you make of Esme and Lucas."

"They seem nice, I haven't spoken to them long enough to form an opinion, why, what do you think?"

"They seem nice, normal really. They argue a lot though, which I'm not used to and the boys are rather loud."

"You should be used to that, I mean, you had boys yourself, it can't be that different."

"Yes, I suppose, but you forget what it's like. I've kind of got used to them staying locked in their rooms with only a computer to entertain them. I've forgotten boys like to play outside when they're younger."

I nod and then remember what I wanted to tell her. "Talking of being locked away in your room, what do you make of that house around the corner, you know, the one with the pretty pink door."

"Why?"

"I don't know, it's just that it always seems deserted from the front, as if there's no one home and yet the window is always open at the back. I saw the man who lives there the other morning and he was a little strange if I'm honest."

"How strange?" Nancy looks interested and I shake my head. "I'm not sure. It was early and he was heading home, probably from the night shift. I engaged him in conversation, but he wasn't interested."

"He was probably tired."

"Maybe but he didn't look as if he'd been up all night. He looked as if he was heading off to work rather than from it."

"How can you tell?"

"Oh, I can tell a lot just by looking at a person. It's what I do, study people for a living to test reactions and build a picture of a person without them realising it. Well, as I said, he was heading home and I invited him over for drinks one evening with his wife, to meet everyone."

"What did he say?" Nancy looks intrigued and I shrug. "Said he wasn't interested. He told me he was a loner and liked to keep himself to himself. He also told me he wasn't married, but he was wearing a wedding ring."

"So, he's probably divorced, or separated."

"And still wears his ring, I'm not so sure. He was also carrying a bag of what appeared to be groceries."

"Maybe he did the shopping on the way home."

"He could have I suppose, but it just didn't really add up."

Sandra interrupts us and says loudly, "Grab your drinks please and follow me. We will all take a seat in the living room and Keith can run through a few things."

As she moves off, I whisper, "Kill me now."

Nancy grins and promptly refills both our glasses. "We'll need this."

We head into their large living room and I note the antique furniture with disdain and whisper, "It's like Miss Havisham's front parlour, goodness, I think I've gone back in time."

Nancy giggles and Liam shouts at me from across the room. "Jas, I've saved you a seat."

Under my breath, I whisper, "He's only done that so he can make me answer any awkward questions. That man's a master at dodging a bullet."

Nancy giggles and sits beside Adrian, and I note he looks as interested to be here as the rest of us.

Sandra claps her hands and says loudly, "I would like to take this opportunity to welcome our new neighbours Esme and Lucas. Now, as is customary on these occasions, please stand and tell us your potted history."

I daren't look at anyone. What the hell, since when did we divulge our potted histories as she put it? Esme looks shocked and Lucas uncomfortable and to be honest, if I were them, I'd invent a babysitter problem and get the hell out here but Esme stands and blushes a little as she says nervously, "Well, um, yes, thank you, Sandra. Well, as you know, I'm Esme Williams and this is my husband Lucas. We moved from Streatham with our two boys Archie and Billy, not forgetting our fur baby Pixie."

Liam mutters under his breath and I elbow him sharply in the side, maintaining an interested smile on my face.

Lucas looks uncomfortable as Esme says loudly, "Um, Lucas works long hours as a mechanical engineer and I am employed as a full-time mum, although I am actively seeking part time work."

"What did you used to do?"

Sandra interrupts and I see a flush break across Esme's face as she says, Retail supervision, mainly."

"What does that mean?"

I want to punch Sandra because it's obvious Esme feels uncomfortable and so I go to her rescue and say brightly, "Well, whatever it means, it sounds exciting, unlike my own job where I get to defend useless criminals who deserve the electric chair more than a fair trial."

I take a swig of my wine and there's an awkward silence before Nancy says with interest, "What are you working on at the moment, anything you can talk about?"

"Not really, it's all top secret and if I tell you, I would have to kill you after."

Sandra looks astonished and the curiosity in her eyes makes me smile inside. Of course, I could tell them little bits of what I do, but it's much more fun watching Sandra hate the fact she can't discover the juicy gossip for herself. This time Liam nudges me and I feel bad. I've always been the same. People rub me up the wrong way and I go in for the kill. I try to make them uncomfortable and I sometimes forget it's not appropriate. Liam looks at Esme and Lucas and says loudly, "Jasmine and I moved in a few months ago and I work in the building trade. I own a small yard near Brighton and business is good. Jasmine's a lawyer in London and work consumes her life, so what little time she has, I dominate it, isn't that right babe?"

He winks and throws me a lascivious look that I know is purely for Sandra's benefit and I rise to the challenge, rubbing his knee and saying flirtatiously, "Hush, don't tell them our secrets, babe, well, maybe not yet, anyway. You never know, some of them may like to play the same games."

I almost laugh out loud at the look that passes between Sandra and Keith, and the astonishment in Esme's eyes brings out the devil in me. I know that Sandra and Keith think we're a couple of swingers and I'm keen to build on that. I'll fill Esme and Lucas in later on and smirk as Nancy catches my eye and shakes her head, grinning as she says loudly, "Um, yes, well, as you know, Adrian and I moved from Norfolk because of work commitments. Adrian secured a position heading up a new operation at the

Phoenix group near Lewes. We've moved a lot over the years and so I don't work, preferring instead to make a happy home for him to come home every night."

Sandra looks as if she wants to adopt Nancy because she obviously approves of everything she does because they are similar in a lot of ways, although I know they are different in the ones that count.

Nancy has become a good friend to me and the more I've got to know her, the more I understand how underestimated she is. Adrian may bring home the bacon as they say, but Nancy rules the roost. She is a force to be reckoned with, and if anyone's in charge in that household, it's her.

Sandra nods and then stands as if she's addressing an auditorium and I stifle a grin as she claps her hands and says regally, "My husband and I took the extremely hard decision to downsize from our rather large estate in Surrey."

I stare at her incredulously as she wipes an imaginary tear from her eye and sniffs, "It was the hardest decision we ever had to make because we were pillars of the community and in huge social demand."

"Why did you move then?"

I resist yawning and if looks could kill, Sandra would be up for murder as she glares and says tightly, "Personal reasons that I don't want to go into now."

Once again, Liam nudges me and I take another swig of my wine, wishing I could just close my eyes and sleep through this whole debacle. I can't remember the last time I had over four hours sleep and it's taking its toll.

Reaching inside my pocket, I slip another pill from the packet and surreptitiously take it with another swig of my wine. I know I'm walking a fine line here, but I rely on my pills to keep me awake because I need to get through this case before I can think of a normal sleep pattern.

Liam stiffens beside me and I know he noticed, making

me feel annoyed with myself. I promised him I would stop taking them and now we'll have the usual argument when we get home.

Great, the only promise I'm on tonight, is the one that will have me backed into a corner while he shouts at me, probably ending with me dissolving into hysterics and promising to change right before we have make-up sex.

Keith stands and my heart sinks as I see him wielding his usual clipboard and I watch as he perches his tortoiseshell glasses on the end of his nose and says in his nasal voice, "Now that you're all here, I wonder if I can sign you up to sit on the neighbourhood committee. I am chairman and Sandra sees to the refreshment and social side of things. We need a secretary, a treasurer and active committee members. Esme, can I count on you?"

He turns to her first which gives the rest of us time to come up with an excuse and she stares at him like a deer caught in a hunter's sight. "Oh, um…"

"Of course, she'll sign up, what else does she have to do?"

Sandra butts in without giving Esme a chance to decide for herself, and Keith nods and reaches behind him.

"Good, then your first job will be to deliver these leaflets around the development, inviting the residents to a meeting here two weeks from today."

Esme takes the wad of leaflets looking slightly stunned but I have no time to commiserate because Keith turns to us and says firmly, "Jasmine, you will be our legal expert who will advise on a free of charge basis, should the need arise."

I open my mouth to tell him where to shove my advice and Liam blurts, "Of course, no problem."

I glare at him and then grin as Keith says, "Liam, you can assist me with the neighbourhood watch project. There is a meeting in town on the subject that we will attend together next Thursday evening."

Without stopping for breath, he says, "Nancy and Adrian, you can assist and Nancy, I feel as if you have time to take on the role of Treasurer. You possess all the qualities and it would be churlish of you to refuse."

Now I know the real reason we were invited this evening. We've been trapped and played, and if I wasn't so angry, I would be suitably impressed. Yes, the Wickham's are a force to be reckoned with and I need to be one step ahead of them because as sure as I want to be anywhere but here, they've got us all over a barrel.

CHAPTER 14

LOLA

I'm so frightened. Ever since Mr Evans left this morning, I've been trying to think of a way out of here. What happened in this room earlier has changed everything. The way he looked at me, the menace in his eyes and the realisation that he's dangerous has caused me to completely re-think my situation.

I need to get out—but how?

I'm a victim of my gullibility, and I wonder if my father knows by now. I shiver as I think about the picture Mr Evans took of me. My face burns and my body heats as I imagine how he'll feel when he sees me so vulnerable and afraid. This is all wrong and the more I think about it, the more I see this was never right. If these men are from the police, why lock me in this room like a prisoner? Why not let me have the run of the house and why deposit bags of food instead of allowing me to fix my own meal?

All day long I worry about him returning. Normal life goes on all around me and I look enviously at people who don't know the horror being played out a few feet away.

Would they help me, or would they look away? I'm not sure because I know a lot about people looking away.

My childhood wasn't the same as those boys who live opposite. A pleasant garden to play in, toys and freedom. It scared my father to let me out because our neighbourhood was the sort of place you sprinted to your flat and bolted the door against people who wanted everything you have. Drugs, prostitution, and poverty. They were normal in Triton towers and the screams mingled with the sirens as yet another body was spirited away, another investigation launched and another life ruined.

It's why we came to Brighton. It's why my father did what he did to ensure our safety, and it's why I'm sitting here now. He went against the code. He stepped outside the lines drawn by society and dared to stand up to the bullies.

What he saw bought us our freedom, but that's a joke because there is no freedom for either of us—not yet. Not unless he plays his part and delivers on his promise, then they will deliver on theirs. A new identity, a new home, a new life, far away from the desperate one we've run screaming from. But now everything's changed because of him—Mr Evans. He looked at me as if I was dirt under his shoe. Disposable and a pawn in a dangerous game. The thought of my father seeing me stripped and vulnerable makes the tears fall and the shame set in. I'm not stupid, I know how these things work, I've lived among it all my life.

I heard the whispers in the hallways at the local comprehensive. Girls spoke of parties they were taken to in exchange for money, drugs and a little affection where they never had it before. I listened eagerly as they giggled in the girl's toilet. Speaking of things that would make your hair curl and your heart almost give out. The only thing girls had in my school of any value was their body, and there were endless chances to use it for monetary gain. A ticket out of hell by selling their souls to the devil. It happened—a lot, and I avoided it myself. It wasn't for me and yet here I am, waiting for Mr Evans because the look in his eye told me my fate had been sealed. That room with the camera, the black sheet on the bed, I knew as soon as I saw it, this is no safe house.

Darkness falls and my stomach growls, reminding me my body continues to operate even though my mind is scrambled. The creaking of the garage door lifting alerts me to the fact he's back and my heart races so fast I'm hopeful on it giving out on me.

Clutching my hoodie tightly around me, I almost hyperventilate as I hear the dull echo of his footsteps on the wooden floor below. Then it changes as his feet hit the carpeted steps of the staircase, bringing him closer, bringing my situation to a head.

My mouth goes dry as I hear the key in the lock and blind panic sets in as it inches open and he slides in, filling the space with threat and terror.

"Here." He throws the bag at me and instinctively my arms reach out to catch it and he says in a dull voice, "I've no time for you tonight, so be grateful I'm feeling in a good mood."

He turns away and I stare after him in surprise. Thank God, he's leaving.

Just before the door closes, I hear another sound, a muffled groan and the sound of movement below and I strain to listen as the door slams shut behind him, effectively cutting off any sound.

Quickly, I move to the door and press my ear to the wood and listen for any sign we are not alone.

Muffled voices reach me and I press my ear to the crack under the door to listen.

Whoever is here is whispering because there is more than Mr Evans out there.

The sound increases as whoever's downstairs makes their way upstairs and I make out a few words, "Hurry!"

Somebody groans and I hear an object being dragged and then a door slams.

There are voices from down the hall but that's all I hear and I wonder what's going on.

I'm not sure how long I sit by the door, but it feels like hours as I listen for anything that will enlighten me. Then I hear footsteps heading my way and I race and stand by the window, nervously playing with my fingers as the key turns once again.

Mr Evans heads into the room looking as if he's run a marathon. Gone is the self-assured detective with no emotion, and in its place is a man on the edge of something I can't quite place.

He looks at me with an interest I hoped would have gone away and says darkly, "Move away from the window."

Nervously, I step to the side and he snarls, "You know the rules, you stay hidden and if anyone sees you, you may as well be dead. Don't make me handcuff you to the bed because I'm starting to think that's the best idea."

He advances towards me and I shrink under his lustful gaze because there is interest in his eyes as they burn right through my soul, stripping me of any dignity I have as his intentions become clear.

As he reaches me, he grabs my wrist and pulls me roughly against him and I smell sweat mixed with alcohol and a scent I can't place. I want to wrinkle my nose in disgust because it's a pungent odour that I've never smelt before and as his arm hooks around my waist, he pulls me against his body and growls, "I'm getting tired of this shit. Your father is not playing by the rules, and so I think it's time we do the same."

His hand moves lower and he grabs me hard and growls, "I'm done with this. My patience is wearing thin. If your father doesn't cooperate, then this ass is mine. I will teach him not to mess with me and you will pay the price for his mistake. I'm almost tempted to show you what that means right now, but I have a job to do and don't have the time."

Before the last word leaves his lips, I hear the distinct sound of someone moaning further down the hall and his head whips towards the door and he says irritably, "Great, that's all I need."

He pushes me away and says roughly, "Our visitor is waking up, that's very inconvenient."

"Our visitor?"

My voice shakes and he laughs dully, "Yes, the newest addition to our happy house. Unlike you though, she won't be staying."

He moves away and then something makes him stop and as the moans increase, he turns and I see a wicked glint in his eye.

"Do you want to come and say hi?"

He holds out his hand and I shrink against the wall, fearful of what I may find.

In two steps he crosses the room and grabs my hand, roughly pulling me after him and as I stumble, he wrenches my arm causing me to bite my lip as I feel the pain.

As we head towards the room I went to yesterday, I struggle to breathe as the moans intensify and as he pushes open the door, I see the room bathed in artificial light that almost blinds me and then as my eyes adjust, the fear strikes an arrow to my heart as I see a girl tied to the bed, naked and bruised. She is blindfolded and gagged and her legs and arms are tied to each bedpost and she moans in pain.

The video is running and trained on her and Mr Evans pulls my head around roughly to look at her and whispers,

"This is what happens to girls who disobey me. This is what will happen to you if your father doesn't play ball, and this is how you'll end up if you try to escape. Stay away from the window, keep your mouth shut and you may just escape this fate. Put one foot wrong and your punishment will be a lot worse."

The tears blind me as I realise something I suppose I've always known. I'm not safe at all, Mr Evans isn't a policeman and this place isn't a safe house and if I'm to stand any chance of surviving, I need to escape and fast.

CHAPTER 15

JASMINE

"Do you know what Liam; nothing ever happens here, and that's what I love about this place."

The rustle of the Sunday papers on the bed, remind me today is a day of rest and personal indulgence.

Spending the morning in bed with Liam is no hardship and I just wish we could enjoy more days like this because it's becoming increasingly obvious my working life is spiralling out of control.

His bare leg brushes against mine and my heart flutters. He turns and sweeps the papers to the floor and growls, "I'm making the most of having you here, you know things have to change, don't you?"

"Hush."

I place my finger on his lips and say softly, "Not today, let's just enjoy a moment when nothing else matters but us."

The love that burns in his eyes makes everything better as he crushes his lips to mine and I taste perfection. Everything was worth it, the sacrifice, the arguments, the loss, it was all worth it because we have each other and need nothing more than that.

But we do.

I ignore that voice in my head that won't go away and set my mind to pleasure instead. We will deal with the rest later, it's this moment that counts and I'm selfish for a reason because if I let the darkness in, it will destroy us in a heartbeat.

It's lunchtime before we roll out of bed and after a leisurely shower head off for a walk to the local pub for some Sunday lunch. It's a beautiful day and relaxing in the local beer garden seems like pure bliss to me right now and I can't wait to eat something nice. Skipping breakfast was a big mistake because eating is suddenly the most important thing on my mind and so, we set off at a brisk pace.

Almost as soon as we step foot outside the door, I hear a loud, "Good afternoon."

Looking up, I groan as I see Keith dead-heading his window boxes. "Hi Keith, lovely day."

Liam, ever the polite one saves me from making conversation and Keith stretches and looks to the sky. "Yes, to be honest we could do with some rain, the garden is suffering."

He casts a disparaging eye over our own wilderness and says tightly, "Although in your case, that's hardly a problem, it's probably best not to feed the weeds."

Feeling a little sheepish, we crawl past him and as soon as we're out of earshot, Liam says with a sigh, "We need to employ a gardener, either that or try to do it ourselves at least. As much as it pains me to admit it, the Wickham's are right to complain."

Nodding, I look at the houses as we pass and see the extremely well-tended gardens and feel ashamed of our own lack of interest. In fact, it's only ours and Charlie weirdo's house that looks uncared for and I would hate to be branded the same as him.

As we pass, I notice the drooping plants and weed strewn

lawn and wonder if people look at our house with the same disgust as they pass. Liam interrupts my thoughts by lowering his voice and nudging me. "Don't look now but Esme's heading out from their side gate."

I look up in astonishment, to see Esme looking a little sheepish heading our way holding a football, and she blushes as she sees us watching her.

"Boys!"

She rolls her eyes and as she steps nearer, I whisper, "God, I wish I'd thought of that. What's it like?"

Liam looks confused as she giggles. "As bad as the front. You know, I couldn't get round here quickly enough just as an excuse to knock on the door. I've been itching to meet my back garden neighbours , but it looks as if I'll have to wait."

"Why, was no one home?"

"No. I tried the bell and even knocking, but there was silence, so I thought I'd try the side gate. It was unlocked, so I called out as I went through because they may have been in the garden, although they weren't when the ball went over."

"How do you know, the cars not here, they must be out?"

She looks at me and frowns and then whispers, "I thought someone was in. I'm not sure why but I was looking up at their windows at the back and thought I saw a glint of something, you know, a reflection off a mirror or a window opening catching the sunlight. I thought it would be a good time to introduce myself, so I'm afraid I chucked the ball over myself and called out. There was no answer. So here I am."

"And?"

"What?"

"What did you find?"

She laughs. "The ball."

Liam shakes his head as I whisper, "Did you look through the windows?"

"Honestly, Jasmine, why would she do that?"

"I would, just on the pretext of looking for someone. Honestly, Liam, you don't have the first clue about snooping and gathering information."

Esme laughs as Liam rolls his eyes and I turn my attention back to the house in question.

"So, anything?"

"No, although I'm almost one hundred percent positive somebody is in there. Archie told me he couldn't sleep the other night and was staring at the moon. He asked if they had children there because he saw a hand appear through the window."

"A hand, he must have been mistaken, it was dark, after all."

"Perhaps, but he also told me he's seen someone looking at us through the shutters. On more than one occasion. Weird, don't you think?"

"Just a bit."

I can sense that Liam's getting impatient and so is my stomach, so I smile brightly. "I'm sure there's a perfectly innocent explanation about it. Why don't you drop one of Keith's leaflets in and ask them to come to the meeting? That's a great excuse to go knocking."

Esme laughs and shakes her head. "I've tried that already. To be honest, if they are looking, they must think me a typical nosy neighbour. I'm fascinated by that place and I don't know why? There's probably nobody there, just the owner who works a lot. My imagination is off the scale and I should probably just mind my own business."

I shrug and look up at the house again. It stands there like an abandoned wife, unloved, cold and slightly rough around the edges. I can taste the bitterness on my tongue as I feel an affinity with this house, and it's only when Liam's hand finds mine that it brings me back to reality.

"Come on, babe, I'm starving, all that exercise this morning has given me a raging…" he winks at Esme, "Appetite."

She blushes and I elbow him sharply in the side and say apologetically. "Listen, despite what the Wickham's think, Liam and I are not sex pests, swingers, or anything resembling it. We kind of wind them up about it and play on their impression of us. Sorry if you got the wrong idea, we're so used to playing a part, we forget sometimes that other people might not get the joke."

As Esme smiles softly, I feel a flash of something that hits me in the gut as I see the look she gives him. There's a yearning in her expression that makes me hold my breath. Her eyes appear to be devouring every inch of his face, and she can't seem to move them past him. As I see the look my new neighbour gives him, my heart sinks. Great, Esme Williams fancies the pants off my man and that's the last thing I need.

CHAPTER 16

LOLA

I can't believe it. Somebody came. I heard the woman call out and ring the bell, and I swear my heart stopped beating for a second. I strain to hear more but the knocking stops and then I hear the drag of metal as the side gate opens and I run to the window, crouching down so I can see over the windowsill.

As I watch in disbelief, the woman who lives opposite wanders into the garden and calls out. "Is there anybody at home?"

Trying not to look, I can't help myself as she moves underneath my window and calls out again. "I'm just retrieving my ball, sorry."

The football is lying against the back fence and I wonder when it was kicked over. The boys haven't been out all day, I should know because as soon as I hear their voices, I watch them with a hunger I never knew I had. Normal life. A normal family and they don't even know how lucky they are.

I see one of them watching me through his bedroom window at night. It feels as if he is, although I know he can't possibly see me through the darkness. I love watching him though. It's as if I have company and I crave the sight of him.

When I see them playing, I watch every second. I laugh when they laugh and will them on when they compete against each other. I love those boys because they remind me that life goes on. For some, anyway.

As she moves around the garden, I wonder what would happen if she looked up and saw me. Should I try, at least? Call out through the crack in the window where only my hand will fit. At night I allow myself the luxury of feeling the fresh air and pushing my lips to the opening and breathing in hard. Freedom. So near and yet so far, because even if I escaped, I would never be free. They would find me and punish me, that much is obvious. Will I ever be free again? There's a part of me that's resigned to the fact I probably won't. I don't think I ever have because it feels as if I've been running all my life.

I hold my breath until she leaves the way she came and feel the disappointment crashing through me as I realise what a missed opportunity feels like. I need to think about this situation I'm in and quickly because it's obvious my time is running out. Next time Mr Evans looks my way, I may not be so lucky, so I need to devise a plan, an escape plan and one that won't fail. But my dad - what about him? If I run, he'll be in danger. If I stay, he's safe for the moment at least.

As soon as the woman leaves, I sit back on the bed and stare at the wall. Next time someone comes, I must be brave and try to get their attention. Whatever happens, I need to escape and get help. I must think about this because I'm not about to just wait here and accept my fate when it arrives.

It's time to fight back.

As the night falls, so do I into a deep sleep and so I'm surprised to feel a rough hand shaking me and a harsh voice growl, "Wake up."

Instantly, my eyes open and I see Mr Evans staring at me with displeasure and my heart freezes. He's back. This isn't good.

Quickly, I sit up and he grabs my hands and before I know what's happening, snaps handcuffs around my wrists and says angrily, "I told you to stay away from the window."

"But…"

"But what? Did somebody come around here today, or not?"

My eyes are wide and terrified, and I shake my head. "She didn't see me, I stayed hidden."

"She must have done to throw that ball over the fence and come snooping."

Suddenly, he raises his hand and slaps me hard across the face and I taste blood on my tongue as he snarls, "That's for dragging unwanted attention onto us. You didn't know I have cameras hidden everywhere, did you? I told you not to mess with me."

He slaps me again on the other cheek just as hard and growls, "And that's for lying to me."

The tears stream down my throbbing face and I stutter, "I haven't, I've done what you told me to."

He shakes me hard and squeezes my arms, saying tightly, "Don't answer back. I've had it with you, your father, and this whole fucking situation. You're just lucky I'm a patient man because if I had my way, you would have been shipped out and put to work a long time ago. But no, they had to go against my wishes and pussy foot around your fucking father. Well, time's running out sweetheart because daddy's not playing anymore."

"What do you mean?" I feel so afraid, what if something's happened to my father, he could be hurt, or worse, dead?"

Mr Evans throws me roughly against the headboard and my head hits the wall as he snarls, "Your father only had one job to do to keep you safe. Well, that's a laugh because you were never safe. He just needed to think you were. Now he's blown it and we're left dealing with a shitstorm."

My heart beats so fast I almost can't breathe and say fearfully, "Is he hurt, please you have to tell me?"

I feel the blow to my stomach before I register it's coming, and his hand slams against my mouth as I howl in pain. My cries are muffled by his hand and he says darkly, "Word of warning, don't piss me off like your father has, you won't like what that involves. Now shut the fuck up and think about your situation because when I come back your life will change forever."

He stands and then with a wicked smile leans towards me and whispers, "We'll have some fun next time. Well, one of us will at least. You may not find it quite so satisfying."

He storms towards the door and slams it shut, locking me inside as always but this time, I'm left with my hands cuffed together and a huge pain in my face and stomach but they are nothing to the fear that creeps across me like an unwanted virus.

I don't have long.

I must make my move.

CHAPTER 17

NANCY

"Mum, can you come here, please?"

Sighing heavily, I lay the rolling pin down and dust the flour off my hands.

"Mum!!"

"I'm coming, I'm coming."

Muttering under my breath, I stomp upstairs, ready to tear a strip off Ryan for daring to call me rather than coming and finding me himself. If it's to bring him food, I would be wise to bring the rolling pin with me and bash him over the head with it. They think I'm a glorified servant in this house, and I've had enough.

As I push open the door to Ryan's room, I hold my breath. Stale sweat, pungent odours and old food greet me as I venture inside a room he rarely leaves.

"Quickly."

I see him looking out of the window, hunched over his computer as always, but something about the tone of his voice makes me curious. "What is it?"

"I saw something."

"What?"

"Opposite."

"What, the Armitage's house."

"No, that weird one next door with the pink door."

Now I'm interested and head towards him and whisper, "What is it?"

He looks a little guilty and my warning bells ring loud and clear. Oh no, not again, I'm not sure if I can deal with it happening again.

"Please tell me you didn't..."

"I'm sorry mum."

The frustration, the fear and the sheer disappointment almost choke me as I struggle to form words, but Ryan doesn't appear to share my concerns as he taps on his computer and I see something on the screen I don't recognise.

"What is that?"

"It's a camera and a weird room arrangement, don't you think?"

As I peer closer, I see a room with a camera set up on a tripod before an enormous bed covered in nothing but a black sheet. My heart freezes as I see something that is most definitely not ok and say fearfully, "Where is this?"

"That house."

Ryan points to the house behind Esme and I feel my heart rate escalate to breaking point and I can't decide whether I'm angrier at Ryan, or more intrigued at what he found.

He leans back and says incredulously, "It's a sex house, isn't it?"

"Ryan!"

I can't believe my eyes and ears and feel it necessary to explain this away as something ordinary because surely, it's no such thing, not here, not in Meadow Vale and not in full sight of our sparkling windows.

"Don't be ridiculous, it's probably a photographer's

studio, the black sheet is like one of those green screens and I'm sure it's all perfectly innocent. What isn't though, is how you got this footage, honestly Ryan, I thought we'd sorted this, what's the matter with you?"

"I'm sorry mum."

He says the words but I'm not feeling the remorse and I say icily, "We will talk about this when your father gets home. Until then, I want you to shut down this operation, immediately."

"But…"

"No buts, it's wrong, Ryan. Wrong on every level, and I thought you had learnt your lesson after the last time. You cannot go around infringing on people's privacy like this. It's against the law and carries a stiff penalty if you're discovered. You were just lucky they dropped the charges the last time this happened and I'm afraid of your future if this is how you get your kicks."

"What's going on?"

Owen pokes his head around the door and sees the screen and his eyes widen. "Wow, let me see."

"Shut it down at once, Ryan, I won't tell you again."

Luckily, Ryan knows better than to push his luck as Owen cries, "I never saw it, what is it, are there girls on it?"

"Owen, go to your room and don't breathe a word about any of this, do you hear me?"

"But…"

"Owen!!!"

I yell at him so loudly the neighbours must hear me and he slams the door behind him, shouting, "I hate my life."

I glare at Ryan angrily. "Now look what you've done, he'll be in one of his moods and I'll be the one who has to deal with it as usual. Now, clean up this room and I want to see the colour of this carpet in exactly thirty minutes time, while I think about your punishment."

I storm out before he has a chance to argue and feel my nerves reach breaking point. I suppose I'm so angry with him I don't even register what I saw. In fact, I don't give it a second thought at all, explaining it away as just what I said. A photographer's studio. No, the most important thing on my mind is discovering that my eldest son has learned nothing at all. He's still at it and now I have serious concerns for his mental health. We need advice and fast.

∽

IF I THOUGHT Adrian would be any help at all, I was deluded because as soon as I fill him in, he is more interested in what Ryan found than the fact his son has broken the law —again.

"It's all a bit weird if you ask me, maybe we should call the police."

"And tell them what exactly, Adrian? That our son is secretly filming the neighbours and we discovered what appears to be a sex room in the house behind us. No, that is most definitely not an option because this is something that stops now. You must lay down the law to your son and confiscate that computer of his. He can't get away with it again because if he continues, he will end up on the sex offenders register and be somebody's bitch in Pentonville prison. Deal with it, Adrian, or I will."

Adrian knows better than to say another word and leaves me fuming while he heads off to deal with our out-of-control son. As soon as he leaves the room, I sit with my head in my hands and try to get my breathing under control. Not again, please God, not again.

I can't help the memory return as I remember why we moved here in the first place. A fresh start, new beginnings, and as far away from Norfolk as possible because Adrian's new job was not by chance. He applied for the transfer for a very good reason—Ryan.

I will never forget that night when Sarah Havilland's parents came around with harmful words and viscous expressions. It turned out that Ryan had been secretly filming their daughter in her room at night and had uploaded the video to his phone and was showing his friends in the playground. It was all around the school and they assured me they would have no hesitation in calling the police and prosecuting him for everything under the sun unless he deleted the video and issued an apology.

If I thought it strange that her parents weren't taking it further, I didn't dwell on it. My only concern was Ryan, and as the weeks went by, the fallout from the incident didn't diminish. He now had a reputation that followed him, and it was hard to shake. What was once a popular student turned into a recluse, a loner, and so we decided to leave.

I thought he had learned his lesson. I thought we were over this, but now it's all come back to bite us because it appears that Ryan learned nothing at all. The fact he even showed me makes me wonder about his sanity. Does he really not know that this is wrong?

Then again, what about his discovery? I know what I saw, and that was sinister to the extreme. I shudder to think what's going on there and wonder what else is going on around me that I don't know about.

CHAPTER 18

NANCY

I don't think I slept a wink all night. I resented Adrian for falling asleep as soon as his head hit the pillow, and even my sleep spray did little to stop my mind from racing. It's happening again, this time it's serious. I know the last one was, but this means we may have to take action because what if Ryan's right, what if it is a sex house? It's a disaster and I must do something to stop it immediately before it escalates.

The only person I can trust with this is Jasmine. I'm sure she'll know what to do, even it means telling a few white lies to get Ryan off the hook. She deals with the law and wouldn't look kindly on his hobby and yet she's the one who can stop this, I just have to trust my judgement on this.

As always, she's left for work before I even boil the kettle in the morning, and so I'm resigned to sending her a quick text instead.

. . .

NANCY: Hey, are you free for a drink later, just the two of us? I have something I need to run by you. It shouldn't take long.

It takes a while for her to reply, but it comes when I finish my morning Pilates.

JASMINE: Sure, I'm back around 7pm. Why don't you come over and we can chat while I fix dinner?

I'm not sure how I manage to concentrate the rest of the day, and I spend most of it baking to distract my attention. I hear Esme yelling at her boys and pray to God they don't end up like Ryan. It's a strange world we now live in that nobody gave me the manual to. My children know and do things I couldn't possibly comprehend, and that scares me more than anything. How can I police their activities when I don't know what they are? They are always five steps ahead of me and I'm floundering in a world I know nothing about. I can't even download a playlist on iTunes and need Ryan or Owen to help me, so what chance do I stand at monitoring their online activity?

Sometimes I wish the Internet had never been invented and children were made to communicate face to face and actually leave their rooms for once. Both of my boys spend more time incarcerated than your average prisoner, and I don't know what to do about it. I've nagged Ryan to get a part-time job, but he informed me he earned more online than any employer could ever pay him. When I asked what it was, he mumbled something about affiliate links and gaming, and I zoned out immediately. If he has money, he spends it on more computer games and software, and I don't have a clue what he does when he's locked in his room.

Owen is much the same, although he does at least have a couple of friends he plays football with occasionally. I am fearful for this generation because I'm not sure how they will survive in the actual world.

Nobody appears to want to work these days, just post pictures and revel in the likes and comments. The mere mention of a job in an insurance company, or learning a trade, causes their eyes to glaze over and all the answer I get is a patronising shake of the head and a slight smirk. Yes, I know nothing about this brave new world, but I do know one thing. What's going on in the house with the pretty pink door is not normal.

Armed with freshly baked flapjacks and a bottle of Prosecco, I knock on Jasmine and Liam's door at ten past seven. Jasmine opens it looking business-like in her smart navy suit and silk blouse. She looks tired though and I feel bad for disturbing her but she smiles sweetly and says with relief, "Thank god, you brought food."

She takes my offering eagerly and stuffs a whole slice of flapjack into her mouth and groans with appreciation. "I think I love you, Nancy. Will you become my live-in lodger and feed me 24/7"?

Liam ventures out of his office and seizes one for himself. "Thank god for neighbours, you're welcome anytime but only with food."

As I follow Jasmine to her kitchen, it strikes me it's just like the showroom we viewed when we looked around the development. Nothing is out of place and pristine, and I wonder if they actually use any of this stuff. Jasmine gestures to the nearby bar stool and reaches for the Prosecco. "Take a seat and I'll pour us all a glass of fizz. It's been a hell of a day and I need this more than calories at the moment."

As she pours us a glass, I feel bad as I see the tired lines around her bloodshot eyes and the worry on her face. "Bad day?"

She nods sadly. "It was a pig of a day, actually. I had a meeting with our client and he gives me the creeps. A pervert of the worst kind and not even sorry for what he did. He thinks it's our job to make his case and get him off scot free, and I suppose it is. I don't have to like it though—or him."

She shivers and takes a large slug of the Prosecco, and for the first time since I met her, I feel a little sorry for her. I always envied Jasmine and Liam. They appear to have the perfect marriage. Totally in lust with each other and living the dream. A nice house, amazing jobs and no worries. Not like Adrian and me, where the passion in our relationship died out years ago. Sex is once a week in the missionary position, followed by separate showers and a floor length nightie. I'm guessing Jasmine wouldn't be seen dead in one of my nighties and probably has a vast wardrobe full of sexy outfits to tempt her husband, who has every reason to look smug most of the time.

How I wish I was Jasmine and how I wish Adrian was Liam.

I suppose I've developed a bit of a crush on my charismatic neighbour. He is devastatingly handsome, well dressed, loaded with money and a decent guy to boot. He's funny, provides good conversation and appears caring and attentive. Adrian, by comparison, appears middle-aged and boring and I don't find him interesting anymore.

Jasmine looks at me keenly and says bluntly, "What's the problem?"

"How do you know it's a problem?"

"Because I read people and you're nervous as hell. Whatever it is, you can tell me and know it won't go any further.

It's something I take very seriously, my moral code, that is, and I want to help—if I can."

My shoulders sag and I notice Jasmine fix Liam with a look that has him backing out of the room with a jovial, "Well, somebody here needs to do some work. Let me know when you're ready to order takeout and I'll take care of it."

"Takeout?"

Jasmine grins. "At least we eat when it's takeout night. In fact, only Tuesdays and Thursdays aren't. Then Liam cooks."

She laughs and I raise my glass to hers. "Respect."

She nods and then says again more firmly, "Go on then."

Setting my glass down, I sigh and say sadly, "It's Ryan. He's found out some information that I'm not sure is ethical, but I can't let it slide."

"What is it?"

Jasmine looks interested and I lower my voice.

"You know what kids are like his age and he embraces the technical world a little to keenly for my liking. Well, to cut a long story short, he has a drone that he likes to play with occasionally."

I almost can't look at Jasmine because I'm sure she's horrified and probably wondering where else he points his equipment, but I carry on, regardless.

"Anyway, it turns out that he filmed one of the rooms in that strange house that backs onto Esme."

"The one with the pretty pink door?"

She leans forward and I can tell I have her full attention.

"Yes. Well, he has footage of one of the bedrooms and it's a little disturbing."

"Good god, they didn't decorate it in flocked paper, did they? That is shocking."

Jasmine laughs and I can tell she is joking to lighten the mood that has darkened quicker than daylight in winter.

"The thing is, Jasmine, it wasn't decorated at all. In fact, the only things in there were a large bed covered in a black sheet with no other bedding. There was a camera on a tripod set up at the foot of it and a wooden chair to the side."

"Whoa, now you're talking."

Jasmine laughs and pours us another glass. "I think I love your son; this is gossip gold. Carry on."

I stare at her in surprise and can't help saying, "But he's invaded their privacy, it's against the law."

"It doesn't look as if they care about the law. I mean, that guy was seriously weird when I saw him but this, I knew something was going on."

"What do you think—is going on, I mean?"

"Who knows but whatever it is, it's not your average evening in suburbia."

"So, what do you think, should we report it or something?"

Jasmine leans back and considers her response. "I'm guessing they could explain that away easily enough and the person who has the explaining to do will be Ryan. No, I think we need to tread carefully and do some investigative work ourselves. Leave it with me and I'll run a few checks and see if I can find out the history of the purchase. That may help give us the answers we need, but until then, keep your eyes open and an ear to the ground. If there is anything sinister going on, we're on the case."

Our conversation switches to gossiping about the other residents, mainly the Wickham's and by the time they're ready to order their food, I'm feeling a little better.

Thank goodness for Jasmine, I can leave this in her capable hands and carry on with my mundane life free from drama and intrigue. The only thing I now have to worry about is making sure that Ryan keeps it legal in the future.

CHAPTER 19

LOLA

All day I've waited, my hands cuffed and my heart fearful. I can't even eat because I feel so sick and just trying to use the bathroom is a feat in itself as I try to get used to having my wrists bound together. Through it all, the thing I'm scared of the most is my father. What's happening, what's going on, and I'm afraid that I'll never see him again?

When I hear the garage door lift, my heart rate increases tenfold. He's here. This time he may not be distracted. Whatever he had planned won't be to my liking, that's definite. Just thinking of the look in his eye when he left makes me shiver inside.

However, as the footsteps on the stairs approach, I sense a different tread. *It's not him*. They are lighter, different somehow, and now I'm hopeful and worried at the same time. Who is it?

The key turns in the lock and the door inches open, cautiously, carefully and slowly.

A hand reaches around the door and I stare in surprise at nails that are painted bright pink and my heart fills with hope as an attractive woman steps into the room.

She looks at me cowering on the bed in fright and a look of distaste flickers across her face, before she shakes her head and looks at me with an unreadable expression.

As I stare back, I see a woman around the same age as Mr Evans, mid-forties perhaps and immaculately dressed in a white trouser suit. Her bleached blonde hair is tied in a ponytail and her green eyes stare at me with curiosity but not surprise.

Closing the door behind her carefully, she says in a slightly husky voice, "He said you were young."

I say nothing and wait for her to tell me who she is and she heads towards me and lifts my wrists and inserts a key into the lock. As the handcuffs fall open, I see deep red marks where they gripped my wrist and she purses her lips. "Stupid idiot, he's damaged you."

I stare at her in surprise as she rubs each one in turn and says as if to herself, "I'll pick up some antiseptic cream when I'm at the store."

Then she looks around her critically and wrinkles her nose. "This place stinks. Has the bed ever been changed?"

Finding my voice, I whisper, "No."

"Ugh. Typical man, live like pigs and act like them too. Never mind, darling, a woman's in charge, for now, anyway, so standards are about to rise."

"Who are you?" My voice is hoarse, courtesy of hours of crying tears that never seem to dry up, and she smiles with a slight twist to her painted red lips. "Charlie's wife, Donna Evans."

I stare at her in shock as she smiles tightly. "Yes, the monster has a normal life outside of this one. We have a home, two cars and a villa in Marbella. This business is kind to us, and now you're our newest employee."

She laughs and yet it has no humour in it.

"Charlie was called away and sent me to babysit. I'm not sure how long he'll be, but I'm staying until I hear otherwise."

I just stare at her and she sighs. "Go and run yourself a bath. I need to strip the bed and give you some clean linen to make it up. This place isn't fit for a dog, and I'll be having words with my husband about this."

She stares at me with a hard glint in her eye and says sourly, "If you think I'm the soft option, think again. Charlie's given me instructions to hold you here by force if necessary. He wanted me to tie you up until he returns, but I'm better than that. You be a good girl and you get your privileges. Try to escape and you'll spend the rest of your stay bound and gagged in the cupboard. Do you understand?"

I nod, prepared to agree to anything she says if it means I get an easier ride, and she nods with satisfaction. "Go on then, scoot and drop your clothes, I'll run them through the machine."

I hesitate and she snaps, "Hurry up, I haven't got all day. It's nothing I haven't seen before."

My face burns as I remove my clothes and stand awkwardly in the centre of the room. She looks at me long and hard and says critically. "You're ok I guess, but your tits are a little small for most men's liking."

She laughs a hollow sound that tells me this is no laughing matter and says cruelly, "Mind you, they don't care as long as they get their pleasure another way. Don't worry, darling, after the first few times you'll get the hang of it."

"Hang of what?" I think I already know but want her to spell it out and she laughs. "Sex, honey. You will be put to work as a prostitute and sold to men for money. Our money. In return you get fed and housed and a bed to sleep in. When your father's debt is paid, you can leave, but just in case you're wondering when that's likely to be, the interest adds up to a lifetime. Accept your fate, darling, because this is as good as it gets. Now go and wash yourself and think about how to accept the situation and make the best of it."

I need no further invitation and race to the bathroom, slamming it shut behind me. There is no lock on the door, and yet the solid wood between us gives me a moment to think. Prostitution, this can't be happening. It's surely a nightmare I'll wake up from and find myself at home with my dad sleeping in the next room. Not this. Not this strange place I've found myself imprisoned in. Surely, they can't make me do that, I'll escape, I'll find a way, I won't let it happen.

As I run the bath, I think about the situation I'm in. What about my father, where is he, is he safe? If I run, will they kill him? It's too much to think about and as I sink into the hot water, I almost contemplate sinking below the waterline and ending it now. That would be the easy way out. No more nightmares and no more threats. But self-preservation is a powerful emotion, and I squeeze my eyes tightly shut against the tears that are never far away. I won't let them beat me. I'll find a way and I'll never stop trying. Nothing's forever, just a moment in time that determines our future. If I want a different one than what's on offer now, it's up to me to shape it myself. I must be strong and keep my wits about me because I'm not going down without a fight.

CHAPTER 20

NANCY

I think I've cleaned the house all morning, wishing I could clean the demons away as easily. The trouble is, they appear to have followed me here and seeing that room on Ryan's computer screen, reminded me it will never go away unless we get him help.

I'm trying not to think about why he does this. Is it just for the hell of it, or is there another, more sinister purpose? Thinking of the disgust on Jasmine's face when she was describing the client she's working for; I wonder if that will be Ryan a few years from now. Why is he always spying on people, women, mainly? It's not normal, any sane person can see that, but is Ryan sane? I'm not so sure anymore. It's just weird the amount of time he spends in his room. He has no friends, no girlfriends and just hides away looking at his computer and hardly leaving. Confiscating his computer isn't the answer because knowing him he has alternative ways to get online and his obsession won't go away unless we break the cycle.

It's almost too much and I call it quits and go for a run instead. Maybe the physical activity will distract me and release some healing endorphins in my body because I can't just wash and clean all day. I'm almost as compulsive about cleaning as Ryan is about spying. Maybe we both need help.

Thirty minutes later, I'm heading off for a run and feeling better already. Physical activity is a great healer for the mind and I plug in my ear buds and set off at a slow pace, not really intending on pushing myself today.

As I turn the corner, I almost stop in my tracks because I see something very unusual. A woman is cleaning the windows of the house in question, and my heart stills as I slow to a power walk. As I approach, she looks up and smiles and taking it as a positive sign; I stop and smile. "Hi, I live around the corner, I don't think we've met."

"Donna. I've just arrived, although my husband's been here a good month already."

She heads towards me and I introduce myself. "I'm Nancy, it's nice to meet you. How are you finding things, do you need to know anything?"

"It's fine - I think. My husband told me most things."

Thinking about Jasmine's account of her meeting with Donna's husband and the fact he denied even having a wife, piques my interest and I say innocently, "Have you been married long?"

Ten years, although there have been a few bumps along the way, one of them recently. It's why he moved here. But then we worked it out and are giving it another go."

She seems so friendly and normal that any doubts I had are pushed aside showing how fickle I am. I've always wanted to believe there's good in everyone and they are no exception.

"You should both come around one evening and meet the neighbours, if you want to that is."

"Sure, why not? It will have to wait though, Charlie's away for a while and I'm using the time to get this house in shape. Men are pigs, aren't they? I don't think he's cleaned this place since he moved in."

"I'm sure my husband would be the same."

Smiling, I wonder what on earth I was worrying about? She seems so normal and has explained everything in one conversation that we have spent weeks wondering about. In fact, I feel a little foolish now and try to make up for it. "Well, as soon as he's back, let me know and we'll arrange something."

She nods. "It will be nice to meet some new friends, this place appears good for that. Great, thanks, I'll let you know when we can make it."

She turns away and I start jogging, feeling much happier than when I started. Maybe that image Ryan took was what I thought - a photo shoot because looking at the woman she appears normal enough, if not a little too glamorous, making me feel as if I need a makeover and fast.

I'm sure she's had her teeth done and her lips plumped. The breasts that strained against her vest top looked fake too, as well as the dye in her hair. Far from looking down on her, I envy her. I always have envied confident women and wish I could be the same and my hand instinctively goes to my own natural, mouse brown hair, pulled back in a ponytail and in need of a wash. My nails are chipped and broken and my legs could use a visit from the razor, whereas Donna's looked tanned and lengthy. I'm guessing she has a varied sex life, unlike my own, which is increasingly becoming a problem to me because I'm resorting to ogling other women's husbands and envying them something I wish I had myself.

A husband I fancied.

Adrian has become more like a brother to me, which disturbs me - a lot. When did the passion die and when did things change? Maybe we need marriage counselling, or sex therapy because my hormones are raging out of control at the moment and I can't brush aside the image that won't go away of that sex room as Ryan called it. I thought about it last night in bed and found myself way more interested in it than any decent person should be. Maybe Donna and Charlie have particular tastes and that's just one of them.

Now I'm feeling extremely hot and it's not because of the run. The sweat beating a trail to my panties isn't the result of exercise. It's the realisation I want something no respectable woman should - excitement and danger.

What's happening to me?

Much later, I receive a text from Jasmine that makes me think a little.

Jasmine: Hey, Nancy, I need to meet up later. I've found something out about that house and it's not good. I can't say any more than that but come round at seven and I'll explain then.

Nancy: Sounds interesting, I'll bring a cake.

By the time Adrian comes home from work I'm bursting with the news, but as usual he's not interested.

"Honestly, Nancy, you must give up this obsession with that house, you're as bad as Ryan. It's none of our business."

I just stare at him, the anger burning a trail through my reasoning and I shout, "That's just typical of you, Adrian. I want to make conversation and you shoot me down in flames at the first moment you get. What if I want to talk about it? Can't you at least humour me and pretend to be interested in something I am. I'm worried about our relationship because we appear to have nothing in common these days except this house and our boys."

My voice falters as I look at him with a hurt expression

and say in a whisper, "What happened to us? When did this relationship fracture because I'm wondering if we can repair it?"

He closes the kitchen door and says in a fierce whisper, "Control yourself, Nancy. The boys will hear and the last thing we need is for them to hear us arguing. It's bad enough listening to Esme and Lucas tearing strips off each other in the garden without us joining in."

I'm not sure what to say because this is typical Adrian. He lives his life in an emotionless void and I don't know when I realised this isn't ok. I know that Esme and Lucas argue a lot, but I also know they have a deep love for each other that is clear when I hear them laughing and play fighting in the garden. Even their arguments usually end up with laughter, and one of them does something to make the other one laugh. We don't laugh anymore, and I'm struggling to remember a time when we did.

I look at Adrian differently these days and think about when I first met him. He seemed to be everything I wanted, and I supposed I overlooked the parts of our relationship that weren't perfect. I'm sure the perfect relationship is a myth anyway and I busied myself with the house, the home and the family. Making everything perfect and creating the textbook family. The trouble is, I'm not sure if I want to keep on trying and have been flicking through properties on the internet that I imagine myself living a different sort of life in.

The single life is becoming increasingly desirable to me because I hear tales from the classes I go to of internet dating and wild times. I sit and listen with interest and then have to come home to this – him and I'm struggling to breathe under the weight of commitment. Maybe our time is up. Would I feel like a failure if I asked to leave? Would I be selfish and destroy an otherwise successful relationship? As Adrian looks at me with his usual disinterest, something sparks inside me and I say in a firm voice, "I want us to sign up for marriage guidance, this isn't working anymore."

"Are you serious?" Adrian's face is a picture as he stares at me in utter disbelief.

"Of course, I wouldn't have suggested it if I wasn't."

"But why, we're fine, aren't we?"

I feel bad as I detect a hint of anger mixed with hurt and I shrug. "It's long overdue if you ask me. Don't say you haven't noticed that things just aren't the same between us anymore and I kind of miss that, you know, the closeness we used to share, the laughs, the hopes and dreams, the sex."

Adrian looks around him quickly and whispers, "Lower your voice, the boys will hear you."

"That's just it, Adrian, the boys never hear us because we do everything behind closed doors and with minimum effort. Where's the passion, where are the arguments followed by passion? It's as if we just exist these days; we don't *live* and it's time we put a stop to this - existence."

Turning away, I grab my keys and the Tupperware box on the side containing the carrot cake I made yesterday and snap, "Your dinner's in the oven, I'm off to Jasmines."

"Again!"

"Yes, again. And don't wait up, I may be some time."

As I storm out, cake in hand, I struggle not to burst into hysterical laughter. It's obvious my little speech alerted Adrian to the fact that something's wrong because by the look on his face, he never thought there was. Maybe an evening spent mulling over my words is long overdue because I was deadly serious. It's make, or break for Adrian and me and this time, I mean it.

CHAPTER 21

NANCY

I can tell Jasmine's excited as soon as she opens the door. She looks tired around the eyes, but the excitement in them tells me she has something juicy to talk about.

She almost wrestles the cake from me and shouts, "Liam, food's arrived."

She winks and I follow her into her immaculate kitchen and smile at her husband who is sitting watching television with a large glass of what looks whiskey in his hand.

He smiles and flicks off the set and heads over, saying good naturedly, "I'll watch this in the other room and leave you in peace. I can't leave without taking a slice of that with me, if I may?"

Jasmine cuts him a generous slice, and the look they share makes me even more determined to shake up my own marriage. I can't remember the last time Adrian looked at me like that, and I'm not prepared to waste any more time entering old age before my time.

Jasmine pours me a glass of Prosecco and slides the cake towards me and I laugh.

"Cake and Prosecco, how the other half live."

"Yes, a little weird but worth every decadent mouthful. Anyway, I have news that's both interesting and scary at the same time."

"Scary, I don't like the sound of that."

"You're right to be concerned."

She settles back in her seat and fixes me with a sharp look. "I did some digging into who owns that property, you know, number 9."

Shifting in my seat, I wait for the results with bated breath.

She leans forward and her eyes shine with excitement. "Well, it turns out it's rented and the owner is a company in Hayward's Heath who bought it as an investment. Our weird neighbour has rented it from new and it's managed by a local estate agent. It's on a short-term lease, which is to be renegotiated every six months."

"Wow, I'm impressed, how did you find this out?"

"I googled the history and then rang around the local estate agents, expressing an interest in renting and enquired about any available properties either now, or in the future. As it turns out I hit the jackpot and was told number 9 may come up soon because the current tenants have expressed their wish not to renew the lease. But that's not the reason I called you, there's more and it's worse."

I lean forward, eager to hear what she discovered, and she looks worried.

"When I met Charlie, it was a weird experience in more ways than one. Not only was he evasive, but I had a feeling I knew him from somewhere. I had his first name and convinced the estate agent that we were friends and told him that my friend Charlie um... you know, the kind of thing and he finished my sentence for me, Evans. Now I had his full name, I ran a check on it through our computer at work. I'm not sure why I did, call it a moment of foresight because he's there—a profile on our company computer."

I stare at her in disbelief as she looks at me triumphantly. "It's not good, by the way."

"What do you mean—not good, in what way? Oh my god, he's not a murderer, is he?"

I stare at her in shock and the fact Jasmine looks uncomfortable isn't making me feel any happier and she says nervously, "Listen, I'm not supposed to give out any details of our clients, or people involved with cases at our company. I can't give you the details, but know he is seriously marked. The case against him collapsed and that's all I know, but that man is not the neighbour you want living anywhere near you."

Her words cause me to panic even more and I falter, "Are we safe?"

"I think so, the only good news is that he's moving on. The thing is, Nancy, I wanted to ask you a favour, well, Ryan really."

I feel my heart sink as I know what she's going to say, and I'm not sure I can agree to it.

"We need Ryan to carry on spying."

She holds up her hand and says quickly, "I know its unethical and against the law, but this is an investigation and we need to know what we're dealing with. Maybe we can harness his energy in the right way and make him use his gift for good, rather than personal pleasure."

I wince at the meaning behind her words and feel the alarm setting in. I'm not sure how to answer her, so say sadly, "The trouble is, we have made a big thing out of this and rightly so. It wouldn't look good if we went back on our word and encouraged him to carry on. How would that look, it's conflicting? How is it good on one hand and not the other? I'm sorry but I can't ask Ryan to do this, it would undermine everything we've told him and make us look bad."

Jasmine nods and smiles sympathetically. "I understand, it's fine. It was just a thought and of course I agree with you, we can't manipulate things for our own gain. We will just have to rely on instinct and observation instead."

She turns away and cuts some more cake and I feel bad. I wish I could say yes, but how can I? Ryan would always refer back to it and think he can do what the hell he likes. Anyway, from the sounds of it, they are moving away soon, so just a few more months and calm will be restored.

~

THE HOUSE IS in darkness when I leave Jasmine's which surprises me because it's only 8.30pm and I worry in case they've gone out somewhere without me.

However, as soon as I push the front door open, I hear soft music playing in the kitchen and stare in amazement at the candles flickering on the surfaces, filling the room with a seductive glow. I stare at Adrian in utter shock as he stands holding a bottle of champagne next to two glasses and he says softly, "Close the door, Nancy."

I do it as if on autopilot and turn in amazement as he hands me a glass and says in a husky voice. "I'm pleased to meet you, Nancy, isn't it?"

My fingers shake as I take the glass from his hand and whisper, "What's going on, Adrian, where are the boys?"

He runs a hand around my waist and pulls me close, whispering, "If you are referring to the two lodgers upstairs, I've given them money to go to the cinema. The house is ours for the next three hours and I intend on spending every minute of them in bed with you. Do you like the sound of that, Nancy, is that the kind of girl you are, do you like to live on the edge?"

I want to laugh but can tell he's trying so hard to create something thrilling and sexy, and yet it just doesn't suit him. In fact, he looks ridiculous standing there with his shirt unbuttoned and attempting to look sexy. Quickly, I take a swig of the champagne and then watch in amazement as he takes the glass from my hand and places it on the counter before reaching behind me and opening the fridge, withdrawing a can of whipped cream. Then he says cheekily, "We'll be needing this. Come with me and let me show you what's been missing from our lives."

I am trying to get into this, but I can't. I want to laugh, not flirt, and that's what's worrying me the most. Do I still find Adrian sexy, I'm not sure I do, but I have to try at least?

As I follow my husband to our bedroom, I feel nervous because if this doesn't work, then nothing will and it means no amount of marriage guidance will stop the inevitable from happening—a divorce

∼

Lola

Mrs Evans brings me a hot meal, the first one I've had in three weeks. It smells so good and there's even a plate of crusty bread and butter to go with it.

She sets it down on the table and says firmly, "Sit and eat and I'll tell you a story."

I do as she says because I've decided to follow the line, gain her trust and then the first chance I get, escape.

So, I nod meekly and start shovelling the food inside, which is probably the best thing I have ever tasted in my life.

She nods with approval and sits in front of me, casually

lighting a cigarette, demonstrating just how much she couldn't care less about me. Blowing the smoke in my direction, she says in a harsh voice, "Your dad's a liar."

I try not to react but feel my heart pounding mercilessly inside me.

"He told you he was keeping you safe when all the time he was using you to keep his own skin safe."

Willing myself not to react, I carry on chewing even though I've lost my appetite.

"He borrowed money from Charlie—a lot of money, to move down here. He was going to carry out a job for us to repay the debt, but upped and left before we knew what was happening. You see, he played the wrong player because Charlie had a tail on him who led us straight to you.

"Yes, it all turned out rather well because when Charlie caught up with your dad while you were at school, he made it pretty plain what would happen to you if your good old dad double crossed him this time. He was given a second chance, but only if we held you as insurance. That tale your dad spun you was to stop you from seeing what a shitbag he really is, and now he's proving it all over again."

I lift my eyes and stare at her in disbelief, "He wouldn't, not my dad, he loves me."

"I'm sure he does, doll face but not more than his own arse it seems. Charlie arranged for him to be a drugs mule, you know, hide packets of drugs in his body and deliver them to Ireland. Turns out your father couldn't hack it and one exploded inside him. He had a seizure on the ferry on the way over and was picked up by the authorities."

I stare at her in horror, "Is he…?"

"Alive, unfortunately. Now we have a different problem because he's in hospital under police protection and knowing that scumbag will sing like a canary. That's where Charlie is now, Ireland. He's attempting to silence your father for good this time, which is why you've now inherited his debt."

"He's going to kill him?"

I stand, feeling such an overwhelming rage I'm sure I could wrestle this bitch to a slow painful death, but she stops me in my tracks by pulling a gun from her jacket and holding it to my head. "Sit down, if you try anything, you die."

My knees give way before my resolve and she nods towards the plate. "Finish it."

I lift the fork but my appetite is lost and as I chew the cubes of meat, they fall to dust in my mouth.

She carries on regardless of my pain and laughs bitterly. "So, you see, Lola, you belong to us now. If he survives and tells his pitiful story, you die. If he dies, you live. You had better hope for the former because what we have planned for you is the slowest, most painful death there is. It sucks being the child of a rubbish parent, doesn't it?"

Before I can even answer, I feel a blow on the back of my head and then, oblivion.

~

THE FACT my head hurts so much probably wakes me, and I stare up at the ceiling as the events that happened earlier come back to me. Immediately, I sit bolt upright and look around in fear but notice that thankfully I'm alone. It's dark outside and the room is pitch black, but my eyes quickly adjust and I can tell I'm alone.

My legs shake as I swing them over the bed and feel my way to the door. I turn the handle but as usual it's locked and I feel the frustration tearing me apart. My dad's in hospital, he's in danger and there's nothing I can do about it.

I don't believe Mrs Evans' story. He wouldn't use me to save himself. He just wouldn't. I know my own father and he probably didn't have a choice. I try to think on my feet because I must get out of here and alert the police. I must be brave because he may not have long.

For a moment I sit and think, and then an idea forms in my mind. If I'm lucky it will work out, if it doesn't, I'm in a heap of trouble.

CHAPTER 22

SANDRA

"Is the back door locked?"

"Yes, Sandra."

"What about the side door?"

"All checked and double-checked."

"Are you sure you've checked the patio doors, last time I looked they were unlocked, really Keith, you need to sharpen up."

He comes across and pulls me close. "Relax, I've checked and triple-checked, nothing is getting in, or out, anytime soon."

I nod and feel my panic subside a little. As Keith pulls back, I say quickly, "What about the CCTV, is it switched on and pointing in the right direction?"

"Yes, darling, everything's as it should be."

"Ok. Well, I should get to bed then. I've got a lot to do tomorrow, there's the bridge club and the cricket wives meeting, not to mention we're getting those trees delivered."

"You do too much, you should slow down."

I turn away before he sees the irritation on my face. "It's fine, I like to be busy."

As I walk away, I try to get my nerves under control—they're getting worse, not better, I should up my medication.

"Sandra."

"What?"

"Everything is ok, isn't it?"

"Of course, why wouldn't it be?"

"It's just well, you know."

I turn and measure my response because God knows Keith doesn't deserve the diatribe, I feel like hitting him with.

"There's nothing to know. Everything's fine, I'm just busy. You know me, I like to keep myself firing on all cylinders and if I slow down for a second the rot sets in. Now, can I go please, there's nothing to see here?"

As I turn my back on my husband, I feel bad. Keith tries so hard and it's not his fault I'm so particular. I know this move was for a number of reasons and the main one being that we halved our workload. It was hard work running a house the size of ours, and even though we had staff; it was still a lot to think about. Keith is looking old and I'm worried about him. I know he hoped for a quieter life here, but surely it's always like this when you move house, new beginnings and all that.

As I climb the stairs, I think about our old house and the panic bubbles up again. Meridian House. A large estate on the edge of Kingston. A vast property that took a lot of running and upkeep. We've always had money, that's never been the problem, inheritance, hard work and solid investments, assured us of a life others can only dream about. Through it all Keith remained a loyal husband and I know he puts up with a lot. It's why I took the plunge and move in with the masses. For him.

As I get ready for bed, I think about the neighbours. They don't like us; I can see it in their eyes. We're not like them, it's painfully obvious. Older, less interesting and not about to drink a small off license dry in the name of pleasure. We have standards they don't share, and they look at us as objects of ridicule. I know what they think and it hurts—a lot. I never knew it would be so difficult sharing space with a group of strangers and it is, difficult, I mean because I have standards that have been set across decades but the world is changing and I can't keep up.

I head to my room and forget the last time I actually shared one with my husband. Before we moved here, in fact, it must be several years ago now. It was snoring that started it and soon his visits to the spare room became so frequent he actually stopped trying and moved in there permanently. I'm not sure when our physical relationship stopped. I'm not even sure why, probably after that operation I had when I recuperated for three months. We just never went back to it and now live as friends rather than husband and wife. At least we have that—friendship. Keith is, and always was, my best friend which is why I made the move—for him.

Sighing, I set about my bedtime routine as I always have done and a little more of me dies inside. I'm tired. Tired of trying. Tired of pretending and tired of living. When you've lived the sort of life we have, nothing measures up. These people aren't interested in our tales of foreign holidays, celebrity friends and stories that would make an excellent film or three. They aren't interested and if they only took the time to ask, we would make their lives look mundane in comparison. No, they look at us as has-beens, pompous old gits who love nothing more than moaning about things they don't think important.

Well, I do. Everyone should have standards, and they should set them high.

. . .

THE TROUBLE with sleep is it has its own agenda and when your guard is down, you're at your most vulnerable. I'm more vulnerable than most because sleep is the only thing I have no control of and that's where the shadows claim my soul.

I can taste blood and my wrists hurt. It's difficult to breathe with the soiled rag tied around my mouth, and I'm so afraid. Is Keith alright? He's stopped moving and I lean back to nudge him, just desperate for a response. His groan settles my heart because it means he's alive at least.

They're still here, I can hear them moving around. Heavy footsteps moving from room to room, crashing through our treasured home like the worst kind of monsters. Raiding, ransacking, destroying. They want we have without the hard work involved in getting it. Bastards. How I wish I could defend us against people like these. Security alarms, what a joke. These men know ways around everything and here they are, taking what's ours and humiliating us in the process.

I don't think I've ever been so scared in my life as I sit helplessly while thieves ransack our carefully crafted home and steal possessions that have taken years to acquire. Heirlooms, gifts and extravagant purchases, all gone in a violent night of terror. Keith is slumped behind me, tied to the chair and out of my eyeline. Desperately, I listen for signs he's alive because the blow he took to the head could have ended his life. I'm worried for Keith, what if he's unconscious and doesn't get the help he needs? They manhandled me into this position, but other than my pride; I wasn't hurt.

Briefly, I wonder why the security alarm didn't go off. They serviced it last week. Surely it can't have broken already.

I think I sit bound and gagged for the entire night because as soon as the thieves have what they want, they leave as quickly as they came.

At first, I don't register they've gone. It's a large house and they have spent a few hours here already. Then, as the dawn breaks and the sun filters through the crack in the curtains, I hear the gardener arriving outside and feel hopeful they've gone. In fact, it takes two more hours before we are found by the cleaner and her screams almost deafen me as she struggles to understand the sight she is witnessing.

What happened next was embarrassing, excruciating and worrying as they took Keith off in an ambulance leaving me to answer the questions from the local officers who came to assess the damage.

By the time the dust had settled, Keith was home and nursing his injured pride with nothing more than a mild concussion. Other wounds went deeper though and from that day on, any trust was gone and we lived in fear of a repeat performance.

They never caught the thieves and just told us to make a claim on the insurance because it was doubtful the thieves were from around here, anyway. 'Probably a gang from the north,' explained the police officer as if we don't have thieves in Surrey. I felt let down and betrayed and doubted my husband's ability to protect us. Maybe that's why I decided to downsize and surround ourselves with friendly neighbours. There is safety in numbers, after all. The friendly part is something I need to work on because I know we're at fault for alienating the neighbours. It's all about our standards that we can't appear to let slide.

～

THE DAY PASSES as normal and I'm glad that Keith has something to occupy his time. What with the golf and the committee, he's extremely busy and I make sure to do as much as I can to keep busy and establish a role for myself in this community? It's hard though, I'm not going to lie about that, so when I see a new face I decide to try at least.

As I pass number 9 on my way back from the cricket wives meeting, I see a woman on her knees picking out the weeds from an extremely neglected garden.

As I stop, she looks up and smiles. "Good afternoon."

"I don't think we've met I'm Sandra Wickham, I live in the Wisteria on Sycamore Street and you are?" I stare at her keenly and she stands and nods.

"Donna Evans, I've just arrived, although my husband's been here for some time."

I look around, biting my tongue because this house lets the development down but she's trying at least, so I say magnanimously, "If you need any advice, I'm a keen horticulturalist and happy to help."

"That's kind of you but I'm just tidying the place up. Thanks for the offer though."

She bows her head and I look towards her front door and try to maintain the conversation. "That's an interesting shade of pink you chose for the door, most people opted for green, what made you choose that colour?"

"We didn't, it was our landlord."

"So, you're just renting."

"Yes."

"How long do you plan on staying, to be honest, I never knew they were renting out these properties?"

"I'm not sure, darling, my husband's job dictates how long we're in a place."

"What does he do?"

"Security."

Feeling a sudden interest, I say quickly, "Then I may be interested to meet your husband. We need security advice and by the sounds of it he's the man for the job."

Donna straightens up and I can see her mind working

hard as she says quickly, "I doubt it. He's not one for giving advice, he just does what he's told most of the time."

"Um, he still may be some help, I could probably send some work his way."

I'm not sure why but Donna looks a little agitated and starts to back away.

"Listen, I'm sorry, darling but I've just remembered I've left something in the oven. If you leave it with me, I'll mention it when he comes back but he's away and I'm not sure when that will be."

It appears she can't get away quickly enough and I feel a little irritated. So much for being friendly and actually trying to help someone. Typical tenants, not prepared to engage with the community due to the fact they're not likely to stick around for long.

As I head home my thoughts turn to Keith and my heart sinks. Poor Keith, I'm not sure he's strong enough, which is why I need him to get involved with this community because he needs it more than he realises.

CHAPTER 23

LOLA

Mrs Evans hasn't come back. I've heard her moving around the house, but she hasn't checked on me once. My head is killing me and I'm so hungry I feel as if I may pass out. I tried knocking on the door and calling for her, but she told me to shut up unless I wanted another blow to the head.

Mrs Evans scares me.

The only light to my day is watching the two little boys opposite as they play in the garden. Often, they look up at my window and I wonder what they can see. They are so young, though. Would they understand if I tried to signal them? I doubt it.

Their mother occasionally steps outside, either to collect the washing, or do a spot of gardening. Would she help? Again, I'm not so sure, but maybe I should try at least.

I hear the front door bang shut and then silence. Mrs Evans has gone out. Maybe this is my chance.

Quickly, I head to the window and peer through the cracks in the shutters. Only the smallest boy sits there playing with his ball, and I wonder if I dare raise the alarm.

This may be my only chance, but then again, what if I wait until Mrs Evans comes back and surprise her? I could deal her a blow to the head and make my escape. My heart sinks as I look around and see there's nothing here that's capable of doing any damage. Then again, that doesn't surprise me. It may be a bedroom, but it was always intended as a prison, after all.

Thinking about my father in a strange hospital, in danger of losing his life, makes up my mind for me. I'll do anything and everything I can to escape and raise the alarm.

Without stopping to think, I grab a t-shirt from the drawer and hold it firmly in my grasp.

Heading over to the window, I take a deep breath and do something they warned me not to; I open it as far as it will go and wave my t-shirt out of the window, hoping the little boy will look up and think it strange enough to report to his mother.

Frantically I wave the t-shirt, but he doesn't look up. I dare not call out in case Mrs Evans hears me. She may be around here somewhere, and I don't want to alert her to my call for help.

Despite my efforts, the little boy just carries on looking down at the ground before something distracts his attention and he looks behind him shouting, "Coming."

I could almost weep with frustration as he heads inside and leaves me alone and afraid—again.

Suddenly, I hear the door slam and I almost drop my t-shirt as I hear footsteps pounding on the stairs. Quickly, I drag in the t-shirt and stuff it in the drawer, slamming it shut as the door opens and Mrs Evans stands there, her eyes blazing.

She doesn't even speak, just crosses the distance between us and before I can even react, slaps me hard across the face and then I feel the cold hard steel of her gun pressing against my temple as she hisses, "I've had it with this place. It's time to move this on."

The terror grips me hard as she hisses, "Come with me."

My heart beats so frantically I'm sure she can hear it as I allow her to propel me towards the door. Despite the threat, I think fast because the door is open and this could be my only chance.

If she takes me downstairs, I may be able to distract her and fight back. I *must* fight back because that's my only hope.

Her voice is low and bitter as she snarls, "Don't think about trying to escape, because if you did it will be the last thing you do."

Her fingers grasp my neck hard as she uses her other hand to grip my arm and she pushes me towards the door. If I thought I had half a chance of escaping, I underestimated the woman holding me so tightly and before I know what is happening, she forces me into the dreaded room with the black sheet and roughly pushes me onto the bed. Once again, she slaps me hard and as I taste the copper in the blood in my mouth, she snaps the metal handcuff on one of my wrists and the other part of it to the bed post.

I start to tremble in fear as I see the madness in her eyes and she grabs another set and does the same to my only free hand.

Feeling an immense wave of fear, I open my mouth to scream in desperation, but she stuffs a rolled-up rag in it and hisses, "Try that again and I'll cut out your tongue."

Sobbing, I watch with despair as she fumbles in a drawer and removes a bottle and a syringe and says roughly, "Welcome to oblivion."

The pain is sharp as I feel the needle pierce my skin and as I look at her in horror, she smiles sadistically and says in a low voice, "Trust me, it's for the best, you really don't want to know what happens next."

CHAPTER 24

ESME

"Mum"

Billy calls me as he runs inside and I sigh. What now? These boys and Lucas will be the death of me. I get no rest or space at all and I am trying to complete an online job application for the local supermarket to work nights. I've decided that if I want to raise our standard of living, I need to get a job and working nights while Lucas minds the boys, seems the perfect solution. The money's good and nobody will even know. I can keep up with the neighbours and they will be none the wiser—brilliant.

"Mum!"

"What?"

I try to keep the irritation out of my voice but it's becoming increasingly hard to do because all I want is half an hour to myself before I get the tea, sorry supper, ready.

My youngest obviously hasn't read the memo because he bursts in the room breathless and briefly I wonder if something serious has happened. A sense of panic sets in as I say urgently, "What is it?"

"There's someone waving at me opposite."

"Who?"

"A red flag, I think."

"What are you talking about, who's waving a red flag?"

"An arm."

"Honestly Billy, slow down and tell me what you saw."

"I was playing in the garden and saw something in that weird house opposite. It was a red flag waving out of the window. Then I heard Pixie crying and came in, but when I looked back it was gone."

"Are you sure, I mean, it could be something else entirely?"

"I saw it." Billy's face wrinkles up in frustration and I feel bad for doubting him. A red flag - danger.

My heart pounds as I think about what it could mean. Was it a cry for help, an innocent act that would make me look foolish if I went round there to enquire? I'm not sure what to do, so say sharply, "Leave it with me, Billy, you did the right thing telling me."

All thoughts of my job application leave my mind as I head downstairs. Maybe Nancy saw it, maybe she will know what to do.

Shouting to the boys, I tell them I'll be next door and almost run to the front door without thinking of checking they're ok with that.

I'm not even sure what I'll tell her, but as soon as she answers, she must see the panic in my face because she nods her head. "Ryan told me."

"Ryan?"

"You're here about the house opposite, aren't you?"

She pulls me inside and I follow her to the kitchen and we look over at the house behind us.

"Ryan told me he saw somebody waving something red out of the window. It looked like a piece of fabric, but it was a deliberate act to attract attention. What should we do?"

"I was hoping you'd have the answer to that."

Nancy seems worried and then sighs heavily. "I don't think we can leave it. We must enquire, at least. Let's see Keith Wickham. I would ask Jasmine, but she's at work."

Feeling happier to offload the burden, I follow Nancy to the impressive house opposite and pray that Keith Wickham has the answer to something we don't have the first clue about handling.

As soon as we step outside though, we see a white van heading towards us and step back to allow it to pass.

I see the name on the side which shows me it's a hire vehicle and wonder if the person is moving in like us. We 'moved ourselves' and so I smile at the man who looks lost as he winds down his window.

"Excuse me, I'm looking for Jasmine Davis, I have a delivery for her."

"Oh, it's opposite, number 25. There's nobody home I'm afraid, but if it's a parcel I can sign for it if you like?"

He laughs as if I've said something funny, and his expression makes me a little worried that we've spoken out of turn as he looks at us with a bitter expression.

"No need, I'll just put it on the driveway."

He nods his thanks and carries on and we wait for him to pass before crossing the road, intent on heading straight to the Wickham's. Before we make it there, we notice the man pull up erratically on the kerb, churning up the grass on the verge outside their house.

I stare at Nancy in horror and she says crossly, "How inconsiderate, wait a minute, I'll have words with him."

She changes direction and heads towards Jasmine's house and I follow, feeling as annoyed as she is.

"Excuse me, but you can't park there, look at the damage your tyres have done."

The man slams the driver's door as he heads to the rear of his van and shrugs, "Doesn't bother me."

"Well it bothers me! I'm their neighbour and you should have more respect for people's property than this."

"Well, I don't."

The driver opens the door and I see a strange mixture of furniture and bags cluttering up the van and think it all a bit strange because usually you would expect to see rows upon rows of cardboard boxes instead and an uneasy feeling grips me. Who is this man?

Nancy is beside herself with rage and says firmly, "Please move, Jasmine's husband will be home at any moment and will be angry when he sees the state of his front lawn."

Turning to face us, the man's expression twists in a mask of anger and I get an extremely bad feeling about this as he sneers, "You see, that's the thing. *I'm* Jasmine's husband and I'll do what the hell I like, so if you mind your own business, I'll carry on with the reason I'm here."

For a moment we just stare at him in shock and he laughs bitterly.

"You didn't know, then again, I'm not surprised."

"Know what?"

Nancy's voice is full of shock and I don't blame her as something about the man strikes me as familiar.

Laughing bitterly, he waves towards the items in the van.

"Then let me fill you in. Liam is my brother; Jasmine is my wife and they tore apart our family by running off together. What do you think about your good old neighbours now?"

He turns away and jumps into the van, seizing bin bags and throwing them unceremoniously from the back of the van into the front garden.

I stare at Nancy in shock as the pile grows and she whispers, "I'd better text Jasmine."

Whipping out her phone, she starts typing as we hear an angry, "Stop that at once, what's going on."

Sandra Wickham comes charging towards us, looking so ferocious my heart sinks with relief because it would take a brave man to go up against our formidable neighbour.

She stops beside us and says angrily, "Stop that immediately, you can't deposit your rubbish here, remove it at once."

The man growls, "Mind your own business, you interfering old hag, I've every right to do this."

"How dare you!" Sandra immediately turns red and shouts, "I'll call the police, I'll have you arrested for trespassing."

"Go on then, I'm doing nothing wrong."

Sandra looks at us in astonishment and I whisper, "Apparently, this is Jasmine's husband and this is her stuff."

"Her husband, but…"

For the first time, I see Sandra Wickham lost for words as we all stare open-mouthed at a man who looks very much like Liam confirming that his story could be true. Nancy whispers, "I've texted Jasmine, but there's no reply. Poor thing, I knew none of this. I'm sure this will come as quite a shock."

Forgetting why we're even here at all, the three of us just stare in horror and disbelief as the man throws Jasmine's possessions onto their front garden and then starts pushing items of furniture to the door of the van. Sandra says firmly, "Oh no, I will not allow you to leave furniture, stop this at once."

Looking bored, the man stops what he's doing and fixes us with a resigned look. "Listen girls, I know you're thinking about your neighbours, at least I think you are but listen up. Your friends are the worst kind of scum and don't deserve your help. My brother went against his own blood to take something that didn't belong to him. He wanted what I had and as usual made it his mission to get it. I loved my wife and you'd think three years of marriage would demand some loyalty, but no. She couldn't leave fast enough, showing me that she's only interested in one thing—what *she* wants. Well, they can rot in hell together as far as I'm concerned because he's welcome to the traitorous bitch. They are no longer welcome in our family and have made their choice and now have to live with it. I'm just returning her stuff, so if you have any compassion for someone who has just lost not only his brother but his wife as well, please let me do this and then leave to pick up the pieces of my life and try to move on."

I think every single one of us feels compassion for the man who stands looking emotional and weary before us. I can tell he's upset and apparently has every right to be so. Sandra Wickham is shaking her head and muttering, "Disgusting, poor man."

Nancy is quiet beside me and I don't know where to look.

As the furniture breaks on contact with their driveway, we watch a man cleansing his demons in the most damaging way. It feels wrong to intrude on a moment of revenge because I'm guessing this results from a lot of pain and anger. It doesn't feel right to intrude, and yet how can anything about this be right? Jasmine and Liam, the perfect couple, or so we all thought. The thing is, there is nothing perfect about this at all, just incredibly sad and no doubt devastating for all involved.

CHAPTER 25

SANDRA

It takes a lot to shock me, but this has. Seeing the poor man venting his anger in a situation completely out of control, shocks me because I'm feeling as if I'd like to lend a hand. Jasmine and Liam committed adultery and worse, with Liam's brother. It makes me look at them in a different light, and I'm not sure if moving here was such a good idea. Do people have no morals these days? Is it a case of having whatever you want and iron out the details later? I'm guessing it is because who in their right minds does this? It's inhuman and frankly I want nothing more to do with them.

From their blatant disregard for their own property, to their lack of compassion or guilt for another makes it very clear these are not people I want to associate with.

They've always looked at Keith and me as if we're beneath them. Not worthy of their time and an irritation they have to suffer, when all the time it was *them* who were not worthy of our time.

Feeling sorry for the man venting his anger in the

cruellest of ways, I turn and head home. I no longer care what he does, and I no longer want to watch.

To my surprise, Esme and Nancy turn with me and Nancy says in a low voice, "Sandra, do you have a minute?"

I look up in surprise and see two anxious women looking at me with apparent nerves and I say abruptly, "Only if it doesn't concern the Davis's."

They nod and fall into step beside me and Nancy says urgently, "We were on our way to see you concerning a matter we don't know what to make of."

Feeling intrigued, I nod and say quickly, "Follow me."

As we head inside, I'm glad to close the door on a situation I want no part in and sighing, wave towards the kitchen.

"Follow me and I'll put the kettle on. I would suggest something stronger but it is early and well, maybe it's best if we keep a clear head."

I wonder what they need help with because I'm realising that most of the time, the people around here don't want our help at all but one look at their faces tells me something serious has happened, so I say quickly, "Ok, tell me your problem while the kettle boils and I'll try to help if I can."

Esme looks uncomfortable and so does Nancy, which strikes me as odd because Nancy is always so self-assured and confident. It must be serious.

Nancy appears nervous as she says, "The thing is, Sandra, it's about the house opposite, you know, the one that backs onto our garden."

"Number 9?"

"Yes."

Nancy appears worried and looks to Esme for support, who nods. "My son Billy told me he saw somebody waving a red piece of material out of the upstairs window, as if they were signalling for help."

Nancy adds, "Ryan saw it too, and we were wondering what to do about it."

"Is that it? Why the drama? It was probably someone cleaning and was shaking the dust from the rag. I've done the same countless times. In fact, that's probably it because that woman was gardening earlier and appears on some sort of mission. In fact, I've not long left her, so as you can see, there's a perfectly innocent explanation for it."

They appear uncomfortable and then Esme says, "The thing is, there's something not quite right about that house."

Nancy nods. "Jasmine told me the man who lives there is on their database and is a known criminal."

"What?" I spin around and look at Nancy incredulously and she blushes a little and says meekly. "Don't ask how I know but it's come to our attention they may be using one of the bedrooms for some kind of photography. They've set it up with a black sheet on the bed and a camera trained on it. What do you think that means, Sandra, because it feels very sinister? Also, Jasmine told me the man, Mr Evans, is a known criminal who escaped a jail sentence not long ago and is renting number 9 from that estate agents in town. What do you think is going on because, quite frankly, we're imagining all sorts?"

My head is spinning and I think back to the woman gardening, looking a little strange when I mentioned pushing some work her husband's way. Even then something didn't add up and I can see why my neighbours are worried.

The kettle boils and I set about making the drinks and think fast. They may have a point; it certainly doesn't sound like normal behaviour but then again, it could be and we don't want to go around there all guns blazing with no factual evidence.

Handing them the mugs of tea, I say with curiosity, "How did you find out, about the room, I mean?"

Nancy looks as if she's about to pass out and mumbles, "Um, Ryan saw something when his drone flew a little too close to their upstairs window. He was doing a project for school involving, um, maps and got a little more than he bargained for when his drone went off at an angle."

"Hmm." I look at Nancy sharply because I'm not stupid, and if her son was working on a school project, then I'm the Queen of England.

I think for a moment and then sigh heavily. "Leave it with me. I'll mention it to Keith when he comes home from his golf club. I'm sure as active members of the neighbourhood watch committee, we will venture round there later and see if everything's ok."

They look relieved and I'm sure it's because now they've passed the burden on, they can shelve the blame onto someone else if anything untoward is going on. Is something unpleasant going on? I mean, the woman seemed pleasant enough. Maybe there's a perfectly innocent explanation for all this, in fact the more I think of it there must be because nothing sinister ever happens in developments as prestigious as Meadow Vale.

CHAPTER 26

JASMINE

As soon as I saw Nancy's text, I reached for my pills, my hands shaking. I've just finished a meeting with one of the partners in charge of Victor's case and am reeling from the verbal onslaught of a man who thinks we're all imbeciles, me more than anyone.

I know my head's not been in this case, or my heart and he pulled me apart in front of the others on my team, leaving me feeling worthless and like something the cat dragged in.

Thomas, my colleague, heads my way and smiles sympathetically. "Cheer up Jasmine, it wasn't that bad. He's been in a foul mood since they lost the Sullivan case and is taking it out on anybody that even breathes near him. Just be glad you can escape it when you go home at night. Imagine living with him."

I try to smile but feel a little out of sorts. My head's spinning and I feel as if I'm losing control. First this infernal case and now that text message. As Thomas turns to leave, I say on the spur of the moment, "Thomas, did you work on that case involving the drugs bust last November?"

"What, the one we lost because they convinced the Judge the police had planted the evidence?"

"Yes."

"Why, what's that got to do with this case?"

"Nothing, it's just that I thought I saw the man they freed, Charlie Davis, the other day and he's living around the corner from me."

"Bad luck, I'd move if I were you."

"Do you still have the file, I'd love to look over it, you know, set my mind at rest?"

Thomas shrugs and looks in two minds and then nods towards his office. "Why not, the case is closed after all, I can't see any harm in it?"

I follow him to his office but feel a little groggy. It must be a combination of the pills, the stress and the ear bashing I was just subjected to.

As Thomas starts looking for the file, I take a moment to text Liam.

Jasmine: Hey, babe, bad news. Nancy's just texted and told me Matt's at our house, dropping my possessions on the front lawn. I can't leave because I'm in enough trouble as it is. What shall we do?

He replies immediately.

Liam: That's all we need. How did he find us? I don't think I've given the address to anyone, have you?

I think hard but come up with nothing and dash off a quick response.

Jasmine: No, I can't think of anyone I've told. What about your mum, did you tell her?

Liam: No, she said she didn't want to know. It's too late to worry about it now. I'll head home and see what a mess he's made. Don't worry, I'll sort it.

Jasmine: Be careful, he may be around and knowing Matt, is spoiling for a fight. Sorry to leave you to deal with it. It's a problem though because what if he comes back?

Liam: I'll deal with my brother. You just make sure you breathe and try not to stress about it. Remember I love you and we always knew this was a possibility. At least it's happened now. Maybe we can all move on after this. I must go, I've got a conference call but don't worry and I'll see you later.

Feeling a little better, I take the file Thomas offers me with a grateful smile.

"Thanks, I'll check out his profile and give it back. I'm sorry, but I just need to set my mind at rest."

"Sure, I'd be the same. That aside, it's likely we'll be here well after hours, I'll order some pizza in and we can go over this bastards' good points one more time. If ever I need a drink, it's now, but let's just nail this and move it on because I'm struggling to breathe under the stench of depravity that man has surrounding him."

Feeling weary, I head back to my office, clutching a file I have no business reading. I should be focusing all my efforts on this case and what's happening at home, but something is niggling me about Charlie Evans. He's up to something, I know he is and it concerns number 9. What's going on behind that pretty pink door because whatever it is, I'm guessing it's far from legal.

By the time I pull into my driveway, I'm at breaking point. The pills don't seem to be working and I wonder if I should increase my dose. I know Liam hates me taking them because he's worried they're affecting me. I keep on telling him it's only while I'm working on this case. I need the energy they give me allowing me to work long into the night, but I'm not eating well and drinking too much, which is making them affect me a little differently.

My eyes burn with fatigue and my heart races as I think about Matthew knowing where we live. Will he come back when we're here? Is he watching us now and should I expect a confrontation on the doorstop one day? What would I say to him because the sight of his hurt expression has me reaching for another pill? He didn't deserve what we did. He was always a loving husband that lacked Liam's excitement and flair. He was quieter, safer, and dare I say it—boring. Liam is like a bolt of lightning, a spark of electricity that sets me alight. He knows how to make a woman feel sexy and desired, and I didn't stop to think of Matthew in any of this. I wanted his brother and that's as much as I thought about. Liam and I started a torrid affair that made me sizzle. Life was exciting and I couldn't get enough. It still is because Liam and I are two of a kind. What we have was written in the stars and he's my soulmate, I'm certain of it.

As I settle down to read through the file, I think I'll just scan it and make sure I get the measure of the man who makes me feel on edge.

The more I read though, the more engrossed I get and the work I'm supposed to be doing gets forgotten as I delve into the past of a man who should be behind bars.

CHAPTER 27

LOLA

I hurt all over. I can taste blood in my mouth and the pain all over my body is almost too much to bear. The silence gives me a sense of safety, although as soon as I open my eyes, my worst fears are confirmed.

I'm in trouble.

I'm lying on the black sheeted bed with my arms secured to the bedposts, the same as the girl was when Mr Evans dragged me in here. I'm naked and any clothing I had on is now a distant memory because there is not a scrap of fabric touching my body. My wrists and ankles are cuffed and the camera is pointing right at me. I try to curb the panic because that won't get me out of here. I need to think, and fast.

I'm alone. I know that without even looking because of the silence in the room and the fact I hear movement on the floor below me.

How long have I got before she—they return and make this nightmare a reality?

My lips are dry and I feel weak from thirst and hunger.

What did she give me? Whatever it is, knocked me out and has left me feeling dehydrated and slightly out of my mind. It all feels fuzzy and as if I'm in a bad dream, waiting for things to happen that have no place in normal life.

The windows are covered, shutting out the light, and I wonder what time it is. Straining to hear anything, I just hear the dull sound of traffic from the road nearby. No children playing and no birds singing or dog's barking. Is it night time? How long have I been unconscious, hours, days, weeks?

I hear footsteps approaching and prepare myself for the full horror of what lies ahead and as the door opens, I hear the light sound of laughter as Mrs Evans appears beside me, wearing a silk robe and carrying a mug of tea. She sips it while looking down on me, her sharp gaze stripping me of any dignity I once had and showing me she is most definitely in control.

"Good, you're awake, I was wondering when the drug would wear off."

"What did you give me?" My voice sounds weak and pathetic, which is exactly how I'm feeling right now because the entire time I've been here, I've just accepted my fate with no questions or fight.

I'm a fool. A weak, gullible fool, who deserves everything coming to her.

But I don't.

Nobody deserves to be treated this way. It's cruel, inhuman and wicked and that's describes Mr and Mrs Evans perfectly because there has never been any humanity in their eyes. They are monsters of the worst kind, and they have me right where they want me.

Crouching down beside the bed, Mrs Evans brings her face in line with mine and whispers, "Cheer up pretty doll.

You're going to make me and my husband a lot of money. In return, we will look after you. If you don't cooperate, we'll make it harder on you. Play the game and you'll be treated well."

"Do I have a choice?"

I feel bitter and not prepared to just go along with what they want, and she laughs softly. "Not really, the only choice you have is whether to do this the easy, or the hard way. I'd opt for the easy way because you'll be doing this a long time. Your daddy's debt is large and the interest is mounting by the hour. If you start work sooner rather than later, who knows, one day we may set you free. Stranger things have happened."

Swallowing the bile her words create, I have only one question, "Is my father ok?"

"For now." Her voice changes and bears the threat of something I know I won't like, and I think fast.

"What if I say I'll do anything you ask if you let my father go? Let him live and I'll repay his debt in full. Promise me you'll set him free and I'll do whatever you ask. My life for his, it's a fair exchange."

She looks at me thoughtfully, and I can see her mind working fast as she contemplates what I said.

"Sounds interesting, what did you have in mind?"

I think fast because now I've said the words, it makes perfect sense. It will buy us some time and if I have to suffer a little to save my father's life, I will in a heartbeat. Maybe I'll have to sacrifice myself until I can escape, but I'll need to know he's safe before I agree to anything, so I say carefully, "I want you to promise you'll forget about my father. Let him recover and be free to live his life without fear. Then I'll do whatever you say to pay back the debt. But I want a date on when the debt will be paid. When I know how long I've got,

I'll honour my side of the bargain. But you have to promise me first that you won't go back on the deal we made."

Reaching out, Mrs Evans traces a path down my face towards my lips and inserts a freshly manicured nail into my mouth. I flinch but let her and her eyes gleam as she whispers, "I like the sound of that. I'll put it to my husband. Maybe this is the best all round because the last thing I need is a husband in nick again. You're a smart girl, your father should be proud. He doesn't deserve your love though because he sacrificed you as quickly as he could think up a way out of the mess he's made."

She straightens up and reaches beside her, lifting a glass of water to my lips, which I'm grateful to receive. As I feel the cold crystal liquid burning a trail inside me, she laughs softly. "Does that feel good, Lola, would you like me to show you how well I can care for you?"

I nod fearing the result of the deal I just made and her face transforms into one of excitement.

"I'll call my husband and let him know everything's changed. Then as soon as I call him off, I'll set up your first client. Prepare yourself for a crash course in prostitution, honey, because I'm keen to get started. Excellent choice by the way, you may as well make this work for you, so I think we'll start by setting up your audition recording."

"My audition?"

She nods and heads across to the camera. "Yes, may as well drum up some interest. As soon as Charlie gives me the go ahead, I'm sending you viral. Prepare to be in demand honey because I'm expecting a busy few months ahead."

The click of the camera sets my heart racing.

The sound of the computer starting fills my heart with fear.

But it's the look in Mrs Evan's eyes as she turns to face

me before she picks up her phone that strikes terror in my heart.

I'm scared of Mrs Evans for a very good reason.

Why do I feel as if I just sold my soul to the devil?

What have I just done?

CHAPTER 28

SANDRA

Keith's late. I try to carry on with supper but keep on glancing at the clock on the wall. The hours tick by and yet no word from him. Where is he?

I try to contain the panic increasing as I wait. He's never late. What's happened?

I feel sick and can't concentrate, abandoning my preparations to look out of the window. I don't like this. I have a bad feeling that something's happened. Keith's in trouble, I just know it.

Frantically, I check my phone, the answerphone and our emails, but nothing.

Turning on the local news, I listen eagerly for traffic updates, or news bulletins that may alert me to a holdup —anything.

As the clock ticks past the hour, I pace the floor in fear. He's in trouble. I know he's in trouble and there's nothing I can do about it, just stress about something out of my control.

My heart hammers and my skin prickles with sweat. He's not coming back; I know he isn't.

The tears build and I swallow hard, but a frightened sob escapes as I think about everything bad that could have happened.

Should I call the police, is he injured, or worse? A sharp pain in my heart reminds me I need to keep my doctor's appointment next week. It's been a few months and I need to check everything's ok.

But it's not ok because Keith is late.

The sound of a car pulling onto our driveway has me standing as stiff as a statue. Is that Keith or someone else? Is this part of an operation to rob us and leave us for dead? Are they holding Keith and here with his keys to take what small amount we have left, or worse?

I'm almost crying as I hear the key in the lock and the door opens. My legs almost fold as a foot steps across the threshold and my heart's in my mouth as Keith appears and says crossly, "Traffic's a nightmare, sorry I'm late."

Squeezing my eyes tightly shut, I feel the relief hit me hard as I say weakly, "I thought…"

I see the concern on his face as he heads towards me, his arms outstretched and I fall into them with a mixture of relief and anger, whispering, "Why didn't you call?"

He pulls me close and mumbles into my hair, "Battery's dead. I forgot to charge it, I'm sorry, love."

The relief causes me to sag against him and I whisper, "I thought…"

"I'm sorry, I should have left earlier. Do you forgive me?"

"Of course."

I know I'm being melodramatic and after all, he's only thirty minutes late, but that's all it takes to trigger the memory of a time when life changed in a matter of seconds. Since that day, I've been over-anxious, needy and scared and no amount of counselling has worked. I'm broken because of events out of my control. Will it ever go away?

Keith leads me gently to the settee and pours me a stiff brandy. "Take a sip of this, love, it will steady your nerves."

My fingers shake as I do as he says and he sits besides me, holding my hand and reassuring me with a gentle squeeze and words of apology.

As soon as I've settled down, the fear subsides and I say meekly, "I'm sorry, love. You know I can't help it, don't you?"

"I know, you don't have to apologise."

"But I do, Keith. I know it's just as hard for you and I'm trying, but it just won't go away."

"I know."

For a few minutes, we sit while we both calm down and it's only later after we've eaten and life settles back to as normal as it gets before I remember the visit from the neighbours and what happened with Jasmine and Liam.

As I fill him in, Keith looks worried.

"That doesn't sound good. In fact, I'm surprised by all of it. The people at number 9, Liam and Jasmine and their frankly shocking behaviour. What do you want to do about it because say the word and we'll move if that's what you want?"

He turns to me and looks lovingly into my eyes and says sweetly, "What Sandra wants, Sandra gets, you know that, right?"

"I know."

I smile and my heart rate subsides a little. Yes, whatever happens around us, at least we have each other. Thinking back on our marriage, I count my blessings that I walked through life with this man. Reliable, kind and driven, exactly the man I always dreamed of marrying. We've had a nice life and thought this would be the cherry on top of the cake. Meadow Vale. The place we lived out the rest of our days, surrounded by good people. Safety in numbers and nothing to worry about. Well, that was the plan, anyway.

As we eat, we talk about the day's events and Keith looks a worried man. "It's not exactly what we thought it would be, is it love?"

"Not really, I mean, frankly I'm shocked at the actions of people who should know better, but what can we do, it's nothing to do with us, after all?"

"Maybe but then again, we have a right to be concerned if there's violence in the air. You hear it all the time and god only knows, we know more than most about being caught up in a criminal act. Like I said before, if you want to move, just say the word because as you know, I was undecided about moving here in the first place."

I look down because it's true, Keith didn't want to move here at all.

He prefers our own space, hidden from view with no neighbours to worry about. But I moved here for him and he doesn't even know it. This move was done for a reason because as it turns out, I have an illness that only me and my doctor know about.

My check-up's next week and I'm hoping for good news, but there's a chance it's there. Growing, festering, consuming my body and any chance of treatment will involve a painful process. I'm not sure I'm up to it and Keith is none the wiser, which is how I wanted it. I need to deal with this in my own way and on my own terms. Telling Keith that I may not have long is a conversation I'm a coward for not having. No, it's easier this way. Hopefully the appointment will give me the all clear. It may just be explained innocently away and I'm given antibiotics to take the swelling down. Maybe the cyst they removed when Keith thought I was lunching with friends will prove innocent. A growth that comprises something that will be sorted now it's gone from my body.

Yes, I must remain positive because Keith needs me more

than I need him. Keith without Sandra, Sandra without Keith, never going to happen.

CHAPTER 29

ESME

The job application is firmly in the bag and the dinner is on the table by the time Lucas returns from work, smelling like a car engine.

I wrinkle my nose and pull a face. "Can't you change before you get home? Nobody wants a grease monkey dripping dirt and oil onto their freshly mopped floors."

"It never bothered you in our old house. In fact, you used to enjoy a bit of rough then, what's changed?"

"I've changed, *we've* changed. It's all about bettering ourselves now. You should aim high, Lucas. Look for a job with prospects and managerial opportunities. We mix with high achievers now and need to keep up."

"So, you think your job in the local supermarket qualifies then? Wake up Esme and accept who you are. We're not like them. We don't have the qualifications to compete with them, or the money. We are just here because our old house shot up in value and that's it, end of story, no big deal. But ever since we came here, you think we should be something we're not. These people won't care what we do to earn our money, it's who we are as people that count and you're desperately trying to be something you're not and I've had enough."

I stare at him in amazement as he actually glowers at me, looking as if he hates me. I take an actual step back as I feel the force of his anger completely directed at me and he growls, "I mean it, Esme, this stops now. We are who we are and they will have to accept that. Don't believe for a second they are better than us because that little stunt earlier with your so-called privileged friend across the road, shows me you are way better than her where it counts. So what if they have more money than us? Who cares if they drive more expensive cars and eat out all the time? I don't. I only care about you and the boys and if you change, I may stop caring —for you."

The hurt must show in my expression because he moves towards me and takes me in his arms, saying gently, "I love you, Esme, I've loved you for a very long time but I don't like you very much at the moment. Don't become someone I won't like being around, because I kind of miss my funny, beautiful wife who would wrestle bears if it meant making her family happy. I don't like this super woman who is trying to be something she thinks others want her to be. I love *you*, every annoying part of you, so show me where that girl is who used to attack me when I came home at night. I kind of miss her you know, and this isn't much fun without her."

The tears fall as I learn a valuable lesson. The only person I need to impress is the man looking at me with love in his eyes. The only person I need approval from is the man who smells like diesel and hard beginnings, and the only people whose opinions count are the two little boys who have been locked in their room to finish their homework or lose all privileges.

I feel ashamed of myself and look up at the husband I adore and say sadly, "I'm sorry, babe. You're right, I'm behaving like a bitch, in fact I'm a robo-bitch and you're right to remind me of that."

He leans down and captures my words with his lips, and I taste forgiveness and a passion that has stood the test of time. Why did I want to make him into someone I never fell in love with? Where's the sense in that when I had perfection already?

As I vow to be a better wife, better mother and better person, I look around my immaculate kitchen and see no soul. There is no heart to this place and no memories to cling onto. This house, unlike our previous one, doesn't hold snapshots of our journey, it's a blank canvas waiting for the paint to fall. We will make important decisions that affect our lives in this kitchen, and we won't lose sight of the people we were when we got here. I feel ashamed that I wanted to be anything else and so I pull back and laugh softly. "Do you have the number for Deliveroo, babe?"

Lucas smiles and the sun comes out. There he is. The man I fell in love with, my best friend and the father of my children. Why did I ever think I would be happy with someone who would be a poor imitation of this amazing man standing covered in grease and an honest day's work? I'm a fool and I admit it.

As Lucas heads off to shower and change, my eyes are drawn to the window of the house behind us. What's going on behind those shutters? It strikes me that people who cause us to think about our shortcomings give us the greatest gift of all. Knowledge and not being afraid to stand up for who you are. Learn from your mistakes and move on. Maybe it was bad of me to pass the burden of something that bothers me onto someone else. Ironically, it's the very people who make the most fuss we turn to in a crisis. It was easy to heap the burden of what I saw onto the Wickham's shoulders, but was it fair?

It's as if I've seen the light and decide that first thing in the morning, I will deal with this problem myself. It's time to take charge and not be afraid of the consequences. If I'm wrong and nothing is going on there, I would rather be found foolish that proved right. If I did nothing and there was someone being held prisoner in that house, I would be no better than the person holding them there. After all, true evil is found in those who look away and do nothing to help. I won't be that person and I'll make my family proud.

CHAPTER 30

NANCY

As I draw the curtains on an extraordinary day, I steal a look at the house with the pretty pink door. Is there somebody who's being held prisoner inside? Are they desperate for help and what is the room with the camera for? I feel unsettled and afraid because Ryan is teetering on the edge of darkness. He's shown a side to him that no mother wants to see, and his desires are walking a fine line between right and wrong.

Adrian stands in the doorway and watches me, and I feel a prickle of alarm run through my veins as I sense change coming.

He appears to be searching for words and spinning around, I can tell I'm not wrong as he throws me an agonised look and says softly, "We need to talk."

My heart thumps as I sit on the bed and he crosses the room, sitting beside me but not taking my hand as I would have expected. He falters and seems anxious and I struggle to breathe because this is unusual. What is he going to say?

"I'm sorry, Nancy."

"For what?"

"For not being truthful."

"What do you mean?" My voice quivers and I look at him, waiting for answers and dreading hearing them at all. Is it better not to know something that may break you, or is it best to break and then find the strength to rebuild something worth keeping hold of?

He looks at his hands and says wearily, "I'm moving out."

"What?"

I almost doubt my hearing because I never expected this.

He shrugs and won't look at me as he mumbles, "I'm moving to Eastbourne, there's a flat there I can use until we sell the house and we can share the equity."

"Are you kidding me, Adrian, what the hell are you talking about?" I can't believe what I'm hearing and feel as if I'm in a room with a stranger as he shrugs and says wearily, "It's over. In fact, it's been over for some time, but we haven't admitted it. I thought the new job, our new home, would change everything but we just brought all our old baggage with us. Nothing has changed, just our address. You are still the boring housewife you became and I'm the poor sap who pays for it all, getting nothing back in return. Well, it's over, I've had enough."

My blood boils with every word he speaks. Boring housewife, how dare he?

"Boring! You have the audacity to call me boring? If I am, I learned that lesson from you." I laugh bitterly.

"Well, if that isn't the pot calling the kettle black, I don't know what is. Boring, you're a fine one to talk. You are every bit as much to blame as me in all this, and now you're leaving because *I'm* boring."

I feel so angry I could batter him to death with my fists. I'm so worked up I can't control the thoughts spinning in my mind. Me - boring, he has got to be kidding.

He stands and shakes his head as if disappointed by my outburst.

"I can see you're emotional so I'll just go now. I'll be in touch when you've calmed down a little. You see, Nancy, I stopped loving you a long time ago. I just never had the strength to do something about it. Well, I've found what I'm looking for and it's time to draw a line under this soulless marriage."

"What do you mean, found what?"

My voice falters as I face the possibility there is someone else involved in this. Has he met someone else, is he leaving me for another woman?

"You cheated on me?"

The derision on his face causes me to question my sanity as he nods slowly. "I found someone who you could never measure up to. I found someone who accepts me for who I am and never judges me. I found a life I can't believe was there all the time and even in my darkest hour could have pulled me through. To answer your question, Nancy, the thing, the person, the entity I found, is God."

He turns on his heels and leaves the room, and my jaw hits the floor. Religion. Adrian is leaving me for religion. How can I possibly compete with that?

When I wake the next morning, I try to act as if nothing is different. I go about my morning routine and paint a brave face on when I fix the boys their breakfast. Adrian has normally left by now anyway, so nobody will be any the wiser. I will explain his absence as a business trip, allowing me time to formulate a plan before it becomes public knowledge. How on earth can I tell anyone what Adrian is leaving for? They will never understand, I'm not sure I do. Surely God would disapprove of a man leaving his wife and kids— for him? It doesn't make sense, and I can only imagine that

Adrian is having some sort of mid-life crisis that will be resolved as quickly as it came. Maybe I should invent a longer trip because I'm confident he will see sense when solitary life bites. So, the decision that came to me in the early hours is to do nothing at all and just ride the wave until it dies away. There will be no question of this pulling me under, if I'm sure of anything it's that.

Just after ten, the doorbell rings and my heart races as I wonder who it is. Adrian? But why wouldn't he use his key?

Quickly, I rush to answer it and see Jasmine looking anxious on the doorstep. In fact, the closer I look, the worse she looks and I say fearfully, "What's happened?"

Her eyes are bloodshot and her hand is trembling as she tries to stop it by clasping it in her other hand. Her hair is wild and her make-up smudged, appearing as if she's been up all night. Quickly, I open the door and pull her inside, my own problems pushed aside for somebody who looks in need of help.

"What's happened?"

I wonder if it's something to do with her ex-husband, but she says, "I don't feel that well. To be honest, Nancy, I'm a mess."

Steering her towards the kitchen, I flick on the kettle and settle her in the comfy chair by the window. "Tell me everything."

She puts her head in her hands and sobs, which surprises me more than anything.

"I think I'm an addict."

I stare at her in disbelief as she cries hard and I drop to my knees and take her hands. "What makes you think that?"

"It all got on top of me and I started taking pills I researched on the internet for depression. They seemed to do the trick, but I found I could only cope if I took one a day. As things got worse, I took more and then more. Work was a bastard and now Matt's found us, I'm afraid of the consequences. Liam is threatening to leave me if I carry on taking the pills, and I'd kill myself if he did. I gave up everything for him and what if he's telling the truth, what if he leaves me? I'll have no one, he's all I want, just him. You've got to help me, Nancy, I need to shape up for him."

I feel so angry, upset and sorry for my friend and say fervently, "Correction, Jasmine, you need to shape up for only one person—you. Don't let other people dictate your actions, do them because it's best for you, not them. If Liam leaves, he wasn't worth holding onto in the first place. I'll help you beat the habit, but you've got to help me too."

"How?"

"Make it happen, don't waver and stay strong. Together we will beat this addiction and it starts by getting professional help. Make an appointment with your doctor and we'll go together."

She looks at me through troubled eyes and I see a little of her fire returning and my heart settles. Yes, I'll help Jasmine and she will help me without knowing it. Together we will get through our problems and emerge on the other side better people for it.

I make the tea and try to calm her down until she visibly relaxes and looks at me gratefully.

"Thanks Nancy, you're a true friend."

"I'm trying to be."

I smile through my tears and relegate my own problems to the bottom of the pile.

Suddenly, Jasmine sits up straight and says in a loud voice, "Oh my god, I almost forgot."

"What?"

I stare at her in surprise as she jumps up and looks behind her at number 9. "I found out something that could hold the answers to what's happening over there. Come on, we need to round up the others. You grab Esme and meet me at the Wickham's. We need to agree how we're going to handle this, it's bigger than us all."

As I follow her out, I sense more change coming. What does she know and will I wish she never told me? I'm beginning to realise I like my head buried in the sand. It's certainly an easier place to live, with none of the complications of having to make decisions that could backfire in a devastating way.

CHAPTER 31

JASMINE

The last twenty-four hours have been emotional, tiring and interesting. I know I'm losing control; I have been for some time. I thought I could deal with everything, but as it turns out—I can't. Leaving Matthew was a decision I didn't make lightly because up until Liam and I started our affair, I was happy. I suppose I thought that was what love was, steady and predictable. But Liam, well, he proved otherwise.

Since I first met him, we always got on. He was Matthew's older brother, not by many years, and we shared a quick wit and a love of extremes. Matthew liked nothing more than taking things carefully and slowly, but Liam was the complete opposite and was always arranging evenings out and weekends away doing things like paint balling and skydiving. I loved that about him, and he found a willing companion in me.

Liam had many girlfriends and I always envied them his time. We used to hear them at night when we went away for weekends as a group and Matthew used to joke about it, but I remember lying next to him listening to the sounds coming from the next room. Liam has never done anything by halves, and sex is no exception. His girlfriends always appeared exhausted at breakfast the next morning, but Liam just seemed invigorated. He was charismatic and interesting, and so when he whispered in my ear at a party one evening to follow him outside, there was no hesitation on my part.

I expect we had too much to drink, but that's only an excuse. As soon as we were out of sight of the house, he pressed me against the wall and told me he loved me. I was shocked, horrified, and so turned on I couldn't think straight. My brother-in-law. It was forbidden and intoxicating, and I couldn't say no.

That evening Liam and I had sex against the wall with his brother and family inside. Afterwards, I felt dirty and cheap, but so alive. Over the next few months, we met more regularly and our affair became bigger than both of us. We were on a destructive path and there was only ever going to be one outcome. A wreckage.

I'm not proud of what we did. Tore apart their family and stepped away from the wreck.

We walked away leaving utter devastation behind and have made a new life for ourselves here in Meadow Vale. Liam's family has disowned him and even his mother wants nothing to do with us—him. Now Matthew has discovered where we live, I suppose it's only a matter of time before the inevitable confrontation occurs.

It's no wonder I'm unravelling like a loose thread caught in a door. I'm failing at work, distracted and not playing my best game. I'm reliant on pills to get me through the day, and Liam's patience is wearing thin. He gave up everything for me and I'm scared he will conclude it wasn't worth it, so I must get a grip and shape up because I don't have any other choice.

Now I'm heading to Keith and Sandra with news that will

rock everyone's world. We were right to be concerned and we were foolish to leave this so long. What's going on behind the pretty pink door could be the stuff of nightmares.

I knock on their door, feeling my heart steadily thumping inside me. What will they think? Will they agree to assist me with what I know is the right thing to do?

As Sandra opens the door, she throws me a disapproving look and my heart sinks. I know I look a mess and no doubt the drama from yesterday is fresh on her mind, but I can't dwell on that.

So, I just say urgently, "I'm sorry to bother you, Sandra, but please may I have a word with you and Keith. I've asked Nancy and Esme to join us, I hope you don't mind."

"What's going on, why the urgency?"

"I'll tell you when the others get here, please Sandra, I wouldn't ask unless it was important."

Reluctantly, she steps aside to let me in and I feel like a piece of filth as I follow her into her kitchen. Keith is reading the newspaper and looks up in surprise and as soon as he sees me a flicker of distaste passes across his face and he says coolly, "Jasmine."

I can feel their disapproval which ordinarily wouldn't bother me but I'm quickly realising it does because for all their annoying ways, I do respect my elderly neighbours and know they are good people at heart. I feel bad that I've ridiculed and gossiped about them to anyone who would listen, and as if from nowhere, I say breathlessly, "I'm sorry."

They just look at me in surprise and I sigh heavily. "You must think I'm an awful person. I've not exactly been the best neighbour to you and I apologise for that. What happened yesterday was out of my control, but you deserve an explanation at least."

Sandra shakes her head and looks across at Keith before saying firmly, "Jasmine, your business is just that—your business. Contrary to what you may think, we don't need to know the details. Keith and I haven't lived a sheltered life all these years and whatever reason you had for what you did, must have been a good one. If you don't mind, we would rather not hear the details because we're not people who revel in other people's misfortunes. Yes, I felt sorry for that man yesterday, who wouldn't but I'm also aware there are things that happen in life that are unplanned and not always ethical. Just know we are very private people and would be hypocrites if we expected any less from our neighbours."

I stare at her in shock and feel even more ashamed of myself than I did already. I've always dismissed Keith and Sandra, and now I can see just how amazing they really are. Thinking back on the times they tried to get me involved in their committee, or cricket club teas, makes me feel ashamed. They were only trying to get me involved, and I turned my nose up and sneered behind their back. They have welcomed every person here with their form outlining everything they need to know, and I've done nothing but bitch about them behind their backs.

As the doorbell rings signifying the rest of my neighbours, I vow to change my ways and shape up in more ways than just my personal life. If I could turn out to be just a fraction of how magnificent they are, I would be a very rich person.

CHAPTER 32

SANDRA

As soon as everyone's seated, we look at Jasmine with curiosity. There's something different about her today and despite how shattered she looks, there's a spark of excitement in her eyes that's compelling.

She looks around the group and says urgently, "I need to tell you all what I discovered about number 9. For some time, we've all suspected something isn't right there but brushed it off as just gossip and overactive imaginations. Esme and Nancy have thought for some time that somebody is living there in the room overlooking their garden. The only people we have seen are Charlie and Donna Evans who have a very interesting history."

I share a look with Keith who raises his eyes. I know we have spoken at length about number 9 but knew none of this. The alarm bells ring as Jasmine lowers her voice.

"I found out that number 9 is rented on a short-term lease to Charlie Evans. They have one month left to run and I'm assured they will not renew it."

"That's good then, isn't it?" Esme looks relieved and

Jasmine shakes her head. "For us it is but what if there is someone being held against their will? Their time is running out and we may be the only ones who can help them."

Keith interrupts, "But this is ridiculous, Jasmine, why on earth do you think anything like that would happen in Meadow Vale, it seems a bit fanciful if you ask me?"

I can tell he's getting agitated and I know it's because he feels bad he wasn't the one to have concerns. He's always prided himself on his ability to manage and oversee things and even at our last house was in charge of many committees and neighbourhood schemes. He won't like not knowing about this and so I say quickly, "Carry on, Jasmine, we need to know what you've found."

She looks at me gratefully. "When I met Charlie Evans, he seemed familiar to me. Something about him triggered a memory that I couldn't place. It's only when I started digging and found out his last name, that things happened. I'm not sure why but I entered his name in our computer at work and found out he's been on our database for some time."

Keith leans forward and I know he's lapping up everything she's saying and he urges, "Go on."

"Well, a few years ago, he was arrested for dealing drugs and released on a technicality. His legal team cast doubt over the evidence and insinuated the police planted it. The judge and jury believed it and they released him."

"Drugs!" I look at her in horror. "Are you saying that he's peddling drugs from number 9? This is bad, Keith, who knows what undesirables are sniffing around the development?"

Jasmine shakes her head. "I don't think he's dealing in drugs, Sandra, it's worse than that."

"Worse than drugs, what could possibly be worse than drugs?"

I feel lightheaded as her words sink in. I've been nowhere near drugs in my life and I'm not about to start now. If there are drugs in that house, I will make it my mission to alert the authorities.

Jasmine looks worried. "The reason I gathered you here, isn't because of Charlie Evans, although he is a major concern."

"His wife?" Nancy's eyes are wide and Jasmine nods. "I did a search on Charlie and his wife's name came up with a charge sheet much longer than his. A few years ago, they arrested her on suspicion of imprisoning a young girl in her house and trafficking her for sex."

I feel sick and collapse back in my seat, feeling light headed. This is not looking good.

"What happened?" Esme looks as shocked as the rest of us and Jasmine sighs. "It never went to court. The girl disappeared and with no evidence there wasn't a case."

"Disappeared?" Esme looks around with fear in her eyes and whispers, "How did they discover her at all?"

"Apparently, the girl escaped and alerted the authorities from a phone box near to where they lived. When the police went to find her, she was gone, so they searched the house. There were photos in the file of a room similar to the one Ryan has images of from number 9. Mrs Evans told the police she was an internet model and showed them her site."

"What site – a website?"

I feel sick imagining some kind of porn business being conducted not too far away and Jasmine nods. "There were indecent pictures of Donna Evans and apparently she sells private shows for men online. She earns quite a lot of money from it and although the site was shut down, she wasn't prosecuted. I think she got community service, or something along those lines but that's all."

I shake my head in disgust and look at Keith. "Phone the police, Keith. We need to report this immediately."

Keith jumps up and the rest of us look around at each other in shock. Yes, calling the police is the right thing to do. If there is something going on in number 9, we need to put a stop to it at once.

CHAPTER 33

NANCY

I'm in shock.
The police!
I get an uncomfortable feeling as I think of the questions he'll ask. It will come out about Ryan and the drone; I just know it will and they'll check their computer and find out about the girl in Norfolk. I feel sick as I remember that Adrian has left and yet I can't say anything. I'm not ready to make public something I'm struggling with in private. This is a disaster and my heart thumps so fast I think I'm having a panic attack.

Jasmine looks as wrecked as I feel and I know she has equally as much on her mind, if not more than me. She will also have some explaining to do, and I don't think I've ever admired anyone more in my life. She's a warrior that's for sure and will beat this addiction—I just know it. She's a strong woman that stumbled, and I know she'll soon pull herself together and be tougher and better for it. Will I be as lucky? I'm not so sure because what's in my future is a hard story to predict the outcome of.

Esme looks shocked and I don't blame her. She thought

she had left the drama behind her in Streatham. None of us expected this, not here in the leafy Sussex countryside.

Keith and Sandra are quiet, and I wonder what's running through their minds. This must be a shock to them because of all of us, they have led the most sheltered life. I'm positive they have led a charmed existence and must regret ever moving here in the first place.

I think we wait for a good forty minutes before the doorbell rings and Sandra jumps up to answer it. We all look with interest as the door opens and I see a marked police car looking completely out of place on her driveway.

A police officer follows her inside and I breathe a sigh of relief at the sight of his uniform. Finally, a figure of authority who will take it from here.

He looks kind and quite ordinary, and despite the circumstances, I'm happy to see him. I'm sure he'll know what to do - it's over.

Looking around the room, he nods and says, "Good morning, I'm officer Adams from Haywards Heath police station. I understand you want to report an incident."

He smiles and takes a seat, and Keith steps up and takes charge.

He explains what we know and the officer writes every word down in his notebook, stopping occasionally to clarify things.

Once he hears the whole sorry tale, he exhales sharply and looks at Jasmine with respect. "You have done your homework."

She nods and says coolly, "It's what I do on a daily basis. It wasn't difficult."

Sandra interrupts. "So, what happens next, are you going to search the property?"

Leaning back, the officer shakes his head. "I'll need a

warrant to search the house which shouldn't be a problem but may take some time."

I can tell that Sandra and Keith are unhappy about that, and I share their concerns. What if the Evans leave in the meantime? If they are holding somebody hostage, time is of the essence.

He stands and says firmly, "I'll just take a recce. Maybe knock on the door and suss things out."

I say quickly, "Won't that be alerting them, what if they leave before you get the warrant? Will you get someone to watch the house in the meantime?"

The officer looks at me with a smile and I feel a little foolish as he says kindly, "Let's just take one step at a time. You've reported it and now you can leave it in our hands. If there's anything sinister going on, it will be dealt with in the proper way and though the right channels. Now, I'll take a quick look and if I have anything to report, I'll let you know. In the meantime, just carry on with your day and know you did the right thing."

As Keith shows him out, I say with a slight edge to my voice, "Is that it?"

Sandra looks as subdued as I feel and nods. "I suppose so. Maybe we'll never know what went on there, but at least we tried."

"What if nothing is, going on there I mean, do you think the Evans will find out we reported them? I'm not sure I want them knowing I was involved; they don't sound like nice people." Esme looks worried and to be honest, the thought had crossed my mind.

Sandra shakes her head. "No, the police are professional and won't give out names. We have nothing to worry about. We did the right thing, and that's where it ends. By the sounds of things, they're moving out soon, anyway, and hopefully some normal people will take their place."

As I look around the gathering, I wonder if we are what passes as normal these days? If my neighbours knew what my 'normal' involved, I'm sure they would gossip about me and Adrian over carrot cake, not to mention Ryan.

I wonder if anyone here is normal? Jasmine certainly isn't. I expect Esme and the Wickham's are, but who knows? Does anyone really know what goes on behind closed doors because on the face of things, everyone else seems to be living a much better life than I am.

Or are they?

CHAPTER 34

LOLA

I feel sick. This has been the worst day of my life, without a doubt.

The shame washes over me like an angry sea. What have I just done?

Mrs Evans wasted no time and set up the video. Then she made me do things no person should ever have to endure. I had to watch her 'performing' for the camera and felt sick as she explained the type of people who were watching from behind the lens. Men that pay to see a show no other channel would ever broadcast. This is depravity at its worst, and I have just signed my life away.

The full horror of my situation unfolded in this room and I am past the point of no return. Once I had confirmation that Mr Evans was heading home and my dad is safe, she made me honour my side of the bargain.

I closed my mind to respectability and did what I was told to do. Telling myself it wasn't so bad, it's just me and Mrs Evans in the room. But I'm deluding myself. There are many pairs of eyes observing my personal shame. It's out there for anyone who wants to see, and I can never undo what happened here today.

As the camera stops and Mrs Evans belts her robe tightly around her, I cower in the corner of the bed, chained and damaged both mentally and physically.

Mrs Evans is happy though. "There now, that wasn't so bad, was it? It gets easier over time and you'll soon learn to enjoy it. It's easier than being with a punter but that will happen. We have a party booked in a few days' time, I think you'll make your debut at."

"A party?"

I stare at her in confusion and she grins nastily. "Yes, it's not far and they have asked us to provide the entertainment. Charlie wasn't sure you're ready, but I think after that performance you're a natural. I expect you'll be in demand because of your age and lack of experience. Yes, I think now is the perfect time."

Although I want to vomit, I see an opportunity present itself. A party, this could be my chance to escape, maybe I can, maybe I'll escape what she has planned by breaking free and alerting the police. Mrs Evans heads my way and grips my face hard between her painted talons and says harshly, "If you think you can escape, think again. Security is tight and I'll be watching you. The men who are paying for you will watch you and the house we are going to is in the middle of nowhere. If you run, they will hunt you like a dog and rip you apart, so banish any thoughts of escaping from that pretty little mind because we own you now and you don't have a say in the matter."

Suddenly, a loud knock on the door makes us both jump and Mrs Evans pulls back and releases me. The tears brim in my eyes as I feel the sting of where she drew blood and she moves across to the window and groans.

"Just what I need, the fucking cops."

My heart lifts as she rushes away from the window and snarls, "I'll deal with them, but just in case you try anything…"

Reaching in the drawer, she pulls out a gag and stuffs it in my mouth, tying it so tightly it bites into my lips. The pain is almost unbearable and she snarls, "Not a sound, do you hear me, I'll get rid of them."

As she slams the door, my heart sinks when I hear the key turn in the lock. I strain to hear any sound but can only hear her footsteps as she races down the stairs and opens the front door.

A gentle murmur of voices reaches my ears but no actual words, and I look around me wildly for any opportunity to cause a disturbance.

Frantically, I wriggle against the handcuffs but they just bite into my wrists causing them to chafe. The gag is painful and limiting and it's hard to even breathe against the panic attack that's tearing through me.

I struggle to kick out, or rock the headboard against the wall, anything to aid my escape, but there is no sound at all, just the muffled sobs of my own stupidity in ever thinking I had a chance.

Suddenly, I hear footsteps approaching and my heart lifts as I sense there's more than one person heading upstairs. Who is it? Is it the police, are they coming for me?

The sound of the key in the lock raises my spirits because I hear two sets of voices and I prepare myself for freedom. It's happening, they've found out. The neighbours saw my cry for help and raised the alarm.

As the door swings open, I look eagerly at the person who follows Mrs Evans into the room and as I see the uniform of authority I almost weep with relief. Then my dream is shattered as a familiar voice whispers, "Hello again, Lola."

Good cop, Jason.

Mrs Evans laughs and sneers, "I bet you thought you were safe, think again."

Dropping to his knees, the officer reaches out and removes the gag and I gasp as I gulp for air and he shakes his head.

"Oh Lola, you only had to play along and now you've ruined everything."

I feel the panic set in as he says in a low voice, "Apparently she tried to alert the neighbours by waving something out of the window. They've been doing some digging and hit the nail on the head. Luckily, I was working when the call came in. Lucky for us, anyway."

"Fucking busybodies, what can we do?" Mrs Evans is furious, which spells danger for me.

"You must move out." Jason is cold, brutal and harsh as he rubs his thumb against my lip and stares at me through lust-filled eyes.

"Where, the other house isn't available yet, it won't be for another few weeks and I'm not taking her to our house."

"Well, she can't stay here. One of those neighbours is a hot shot lawyer. She knows everything about you and Charlie and it won't be easy stopping her from poking her nose in and asking for a progress report. If she contacts the station I'll try and push them off the scent but I could be discovered and under investigation before you know it and then where will we be? No, you move today and that's the end of it."

"Bloody hell, Jason, this is a major setback. Do you have any idea where we can go?"

"My girlfriend's parents have a place in Cornwall, a holiday home. I'll get the keys and hand them over at the usual place."

"Cornwall, Jesus, Jason, that's miles away, we have a party booked next week, isn't there anything closer?"

"No, this is the best option. You'll be far enough away and will have to make the trip the day of the party; we don't have a choice."

"How long have we got?"

"Hours possibly. If that lawyer suspects anything, she could be calling the station now. I'll help you get her in the car, then just pack everything and I'll meet you in an hour. I think we have a spare set of keys at home, I'll go and get them and meet you at the yard."

"What about Lola, she'll scream?"

"No, she won't." I hate the look in his eye as he snaps, "Have you got any more of that Temazepam, that should do the trick and I'll help load her in the car. The back seats lower down, don't they? Put her in the boot and pull down the middle armrest to give her air. She can sleep through the journey and no one will know she's there."

"That's bloody great, but what about when I get there? How am I supposed to get her inside with no one seeing us?"

"They have a garage like this one. Just drive inside and she should be awake by then and eager to get out."

"Fine but just so you know, I'm not happy about this, Jason. Make some other arrangements because I'm not staying in Cornwall any longer than I have to."

I watch in terror as Jason takes a pill from a packet and forces it into my mouth. I struggle so hard, but he holds my head firmly and pours some water down my throat. Helplessly, I feel the tablet go with it and then he holds my mouth closed and growls, "Swallow."

As he continues to hold my mouth shut, he snarls, "Get packing, I only have a few minutes before I must leave. I'll put her in the car, but you don't have long."

Then he pulls back and the last thing I feel is a sharp blow to my head and then nothing.

CHAPTER 35

JASMINE

"Can you see anything?"
"Not yet, shh!"

I am straining to see anything at all that will show us we've been proved right. Esme, Nancy and myself are dawdling around the green on the other side of number 9. We saw the officer stop on the driveway and then enter the house. "How long's he been in there?" Nancy's impatient and I say quickly, "It's only been five minutes."

We slowly walk around the perimeter, trying to look as if we're out for a leisurely stroll, and I see Sandra and Keith armed with neighbourhood watch leaflets, slowly posting them through every letterbox, in the vain hope of seeing something.

After about fifteen minutes, the pink door opens and the officer steps outside. Mrs Evans is laughing at something he says and my hearts sinks. We were wrong.

Esme stiffens beside me and says in a low voice, "It looks like we were barking up the wrong tree. Well, at least it means there's nothing bad happening. That's something, at least."

Nancy is quiet and I shrug. "It proves nothing, just that he hasn't found anything. There may be someone there who is unable to raise the alarm. Who knows what secrets that house holds?"

"What's that sound?"

Nancy looks in the direction of the road and as I follow her gaze, I can't believe my eyes. There must be ten police cars heading into the cul-de-sac, blue lights flashing and apparently in a hurry. "Oh my God, he found something."

We watch in disbelief as the cars screech to a halt around number 9 and the doors fly open. Barking dogs jump from the backs of vans and several uniformed officers surround the people staring at them in disbelief. I gasp as one of them grips our officer tightly and forces him to the ground. Donna Evans starts shouting and two more officers grab her hands and cuff them and lead her away towards one of the cars. Several other officers' storm the house and there is a lot of shouting and dogs barking.

"What the…" Esme appears shell shocked and Nancy just whispers, "What's happening?"

Sandra and Keith run across to join us and Sandra says in astonishment, "Jasmine, what's happening?"

"I don't know, it makes little sense. Why have they cuffed the officer?"

One by one, the houses around the green burst into life as the doors open and the bewildered resident's step outside to watch something so alien happening on the doorstep. Esme lifts her phone and starts recording it and I can't say I blame her. We just watch in silence as the events unfold and as the car containing Donna Evans moves past us, the last we see is her furious expression as she continues to shout at the officers. The next car holding the police officer passes and the look on his face is one of disbelief and panic.

We continue to watch and then hear an ambulance

heading our way with its sirens on fully, screaming into the cul-de-sac and screeching to a halt outside number nine.

They must be in there for five minutes before they bring a body out on a stretcher and quickly place it in the rear of the ambulance, before the doors slam and it moves hastily away.

Still, we watch because this scene has to be seen to be believed and as the minutes tick by a different commotion takes its place. The aftermath of a sting that took everyone here by surprise. An officer approaches us and says firmly, "If you don't mind, we would like to ask you some questions, is that ok?"

We all nod and soon the residents are mingling with the officers as they note down anything we have to say. By the time they release us, the number of cars has diminished and Sandra says wearily, "Let's go back to our house, I think we all could use a stiff drink."

∼

WE WANDER BACK silent and shocked, and it's only when we are seated in the Wickham's impressive kitchen that it sinks in.

"We were right."

Esme says the words as if in shock and Nancy nods. "I can't believe it, I never thought for one moment we would be."

"Thank goodness." I sink back in my chair and gratefully accept the brandy Keith hands me and says incredulously, "Who do you think the girl was? I can't stop thinking of the body on the stretcher."

"Do you think she was dead?" Sandra voices what we've all been wondering and Esme says sadly, "I hope not. Do you think we'll ever find out what really went on in that house?"

"Who knows, I mean, it may make the news and I suppose

because we are involved, we could ask—the police, I mean." I smile at them all with relief and raise my glass. "To neighbours and looking out for each other."

"To neighbours."

The words are said with one voice and Sandra adds, "To being brave and acting on instinct and to you, Jasmine. Despite being overworked and going through your own personal crisis, you still put someone else first. I admire you and want you to know I think you're amazing."

"To Jasmine."

The others echo Sandra's words and the tears build as I think about the last few weeks. It's been a terrible time in a lot of ways, but amazing too because I have formed unbreakable friendships and earned the respect of the people who matter most to me.

This time I raise my glass and say emphatically, "To community. May we always attempt to make it the best one possible and support each other through good times and bad?"

Once again, we raise our glasses and as the fiery liquid burns a trail through my body, my thoughts turn to Liam and home.

Suddenly, that's the place I want to be most—by his side, so I set my glass down and say apologetically. "Thank you for all your help, we did this together. Now, if you don't mind, I have a life to get back on track."

I catch Nancy's eye and the look she gives me makes me stop in my tracks. She looks devastated and immediately I know something's wrong. She smiles as she sees me looking and shakes her head, mouthing, "I'll see you later."

Sandra accompanies me to the door and as I make to leave, places a hand on my arm and whispers, "You did good, Jasmine. I'm proud of you."

Impulsively, I reach out and hug my formidable neighbour and to my surprise, her arms pull me tight and she whispers, "Be happy, Jasmine, you owe it to yourself and sometimes it takes great strength to fight for that."

If I'm surprised that the usually strong woman speaks with a quiver in her voice, I quickly push that aside. Today has been eye opening in several ways and discovering that the formidable duo has a kindness to them I overlooked, is not the most surprising thing that has happened here.

As I take the short walk next door, I wonder what the future holds for any of us. Thinking about the person lying on the stretcher, I can only hope their future is a brighter, safer one. Who was the girl behind the pretty pink door? Maybe we'll never know.

～

Lola

I WAKE from possibly the most disturbing dream I have ever had in my life, only to realise it's a living nightmare.

The bright lights blind me as my eyes focus on a room with a white-painted ceiling and I look up to see a brown stain running along one of the ceiling panels.

Where am I?

I hear movement beside me and stiffen, before a soft female voice says, "It's ok, Lola, I'm WPC Harrison, you're safe now."

Quickly, I look in the direction the voice is coming from and see a pretty woman dressed in a police officer's uniform, sitting in a chair by my bed.

She smiles. "You are in hospital under police protection. The people who were holding you are in custody and you have nothing to fear."

"The police officer…" My voice sounds faint and slightly

panicked, and a flicker of distaste crosses her face. "In custody, too. I don't think you'll be hearing from him again."

I just stare in confusion as she says kindly, "Your father alerted the authorities and we traced you to number 9 Meadow Vale. In the nick of time too by all accounts."

"My father?" I feel a surge of fear that she quickly dispels by saying, "He's fine, a little uncomfortable but healing well."

"Can I see him?"

"Sadly, not yet. I'm afraid he's still in hospital in Ireland but is due to be released into police custody tomorrow."

"Police custody?" My voice quivers as I realise this isn't over yet and she shakes her head. "To help us with our enquiries. I'm sorry, Lola, but he has committed a crime that is up to the courts to deal with. The fact he worked with us to locate you and amass enough evidence against the Evans' and Jason Adams will help his sentence. You can thank your father for helping us find you, and he was desperate to help you in any way possible."

I close my eyes against the tide of tears that threaten to fall.

My dad saved me.

He never stopped fighting to make me safe and thinking of the price I paid will be forever my shame. I can't rewind the clock, but I can leave it in the past. He saved me and I have a second chance at life—I won't waste it.

A nurse heads into the room and says brightly, "Ah, you're back. I'll just take some tests and then call for the doctor. Aside from a bit of bruising, you seem perfectly healthy and as soon as he signs you off, you can leave."

"But where will I go?" I look at the nurse in panic and she glances at the police officer who says kindly, "We've arranged accommodation in a half-way house we use, until we find you a permanent solution. You're still a minor and will be placed in care."

"In care?" It's too much to comprehend and I hate the thought of it but the officer reaches out and grasps my hand. "Don't worry, it's all perfectly safe and just an interim measure. You need to recover and not worry about things."

"How can I not?"

The two ladies share a worried look and I turn my head away. Placed in care. My father may go to prison and I must live with the shame of what happened to me.

Strangely, my thoughts turn to the people who I saw out of my window every day. Normal people leading normal lives. They were happy and their laughter used to get me through the day. The world is not always a horrible place and something to fear. There is happiness out there and I owe it to myself to find some for myself. It's up to me to make that happen, I know that now. My father tried his best, but I'll be an adult in a few months and able to decide my own destiny.

I thought about the future a lot over the past few weeks and know exactly where mine lies. I'm going to school, to college, and then to university. As soon as I can, I'm going to make something of my life and become a lawyer. I want to help others who have no hope and give them some. I want to prosecute evil and defend the innocent. I want to make my life count and that is what will see me through this turbulent time.

So, I look at the two nervous women and smile.

"Thank you."

They look puzzled and I smile again, brighter this time and full of happiness.

"Thank you for everything, I will never forget you. I think I'm ready to face the future now, I'll do whatever it takes."

They nod and as the nurse starts her tests, I sink back against the pillows at peace with myself. I'm in charge now and the world better watch out for Lola Miller because she's invincible.

EPILOGUE

ONE MONTH LATER - SANDRA

Today's the day. I've convinced Keith I'm meeting an old friend in town and luckily it clashed with his golf tournament, so I was left alone for once.

I've been on edge for weeks now and the fear of what lies behind the door to the surgery is choking me inside. I could walk out of there with a death sentence, or I could walk out of there a free woman. The doctor is my judge and jury, and I am so nervous I can hardly breathe.

Trying to distract my thoughts, I focus on the aftermath of what happened at number 9 and remember how different things were after that. It's as if the experience brought us all closer together, and finally Keith and I were accepted as part of the gang.

Jasmine discovered a young girl was being held there and was now safe in the care of the authorities. The Evans and the police officer are in prison awaiting trial for a string of offences and number 9 is now being offered up for rent. I hope they are more stringent with their next tenants because the thought of anything happening like that again is too much to bear.

Luckily, Jasmine sorted herself out and has resigned from her job and is due to start at a local company in Brighton. With Liam beside her, they are still trying to navigate the storm their relationship caused and I've no doubt it will be a long process, not a quick fix as much as they wish it was.

Esme and Lucas seem happy and she has just started work at the local supermarket. They have settled in well and their two boys are enjoying life at the local school.

Nancy is the only one worrying me because she appears agitated and withdrawn. Perhaps it's because Adrian's away and, by all accounts, could be for some time. I'm not one to pry though and if she needs a friendly ear to offload to, I am always willing, just ask Keith.

My heart softens as I think of the man I married all those years ago. My best friend and with me through thick and thin. How I hope more than anything this lump was just a cyst because the thought of him being left alone to carry on without me, strikes fear in my heart. It was my primary reason for moving. I wanted him to have people around if he found himself on his own. We don't have any family and I was worried. The thought of him in our large house, all alone, drove the move and I know we made the right decision.

"Mrs Wickham, the doctor will see you now."

Suddenly, I'm brought back to the present and the fate that's already been decided. I feel nervous as I stand and try to act unconcerned as I walk towards the door of knowledge. My legs feel shaky, but my resolve is strong. Whatever happens inside that room will not break me? I will deal with it as I've dealt with everything in my life, with a bravery I don't feel inside.

The doctor looks up as I head inside and smiles a genuine smile that's filled with warmth. I can tell nothing from that smile because I'm sure it's the same if its bad news or good.

Doctors are known for their compassion, and I just hope that's not what her smile hides.

"Sandra, it's good to see you, you must be anxious."

Nervously, I take the seat beside her and nod. "A little."

She turns and looks at her screen, no doubt bringing up my notes, and I swear time stands still. My life is playing out in slow motion as I wait for the axe to fall, and then she turns and smiles. "The results are in and the tests show it was just a benign tumour."

"Tumour?"

I can only focus on that word and she smiles patiently.

"Yes, it's just an abnormal growth of cells that serves no purpose. Most benign tumours are not harmful, and they are unlikely to affect other parts of the body. However, they can cause pain, or other problems if they press against nerves or blood vessels. I expect that's what's happened in your case, but now it's been removed, you should feel normal in no time. The tumour was tested and found to be benign, meaning non-cancerous, although we will continue to monitor you just in case there's a problem at a later date."

"So, I'm ok? Not ill."

She laughs. "You'll outlive us all. To be honest, your health is good and I can see no reason why you can't live a full and active life for many years to come."

Just for a moment, I let the news sink in.

I'm ok.

The relief is enormous as I contemplate a different conversation, but that's irrelevant now. I'm ok.

It feels as if a cloud has lifted as I stutter my thanks and Doctor Keegan smiles warmly. "I'm pleased for you, Sandra, it's nice to give good news for a change."

"It's nice to hear it. Thank you, doctor, I really mean that you don't know what this means."

As I scrape back my chair, I shake her hand and feel the

moist balm of my own tears bringing with them the relief that means so much.

I'm ok, fit and healthy and nothing means more than that.

I almost skip out of that doctor's surgery, eager to feel the sun on my back. I almost sing with happiness as I contemplate a future free of worry and full of exciting prospects. I can't wait to get home to share my good news with Keith and our friends and crack open a bottle of something strong to celebrate getting my life back.

As Sandra Wickham steps into the sunshine, she is the happiest she has ever been.

As she moves through the crowd, she feels like a young woman again.

As she steps off the pavement, she sees only the future and as the bus hits her hard, she dies with a smile on her face.

As the crowd comes running, Sandra has already gone. Fate had another plan for Sandra Wickham that was never going to change. As the crowds cry out and the traffic stills, Sandra Wickham finds peace at last knowing that everything is in place should she die.

One way or another, our paths are determined and we have no say in that. We can plan and prepare the best we can, but nothing will stop the inevitable conclusion of our story. We conquer mountains and live fabulous lives, but ultimately, we have no choice when that life will end. Sandra Wickham thought her life was about to end. She was right, although luckily, she never saw it coming.

EPILOGUE 2

LOLA - TEN YEARS LATER

I feel so nervous, it's a strange feeling being here, but this was always part of my plan. Some would call me foolish, others strange. I'm not sure if this was such a good idea, but I need to lay the ghosts to rest.

I walk towards the door of number 9, Willow Drive, Meadow Vale, and the key shakes in my hand.

I'm back.

I'm here alone.

Marcus wanted me to wait for him to finish work, but this is something I needed to do on my own. I must confront my past and put my fears to rest because everything I've done since I was here last, was leading to this moment.

True to my word, I knuckled down and applied myself. They placed me with a foster family, who, as luck would have it, were teachers. They couldn't believe their luck when, far from being a wayward teenager, I craved their knowledge. I worked hard every minute I could and up until today; I stayed living with them. I look on Carl and Fiona as the parents I always thought I'd have. Finally, I have a mother and what a fabulous one she is.

My own father went to prison for two years but is out now and finding his way. It was easier for me to stay with the Grosvenor's, although I'm still close to my dad and see him regularly.

When I went to university, they all encouraged me every step of the way. Three people watched me graduate with honours and now I'm due to take up a junior position in a law firm in London.

I've come a long way since I was here last, showing what determination can do for a person. I didn't let what happened define me and here I am, moving in with my boyfriend Marcus Fisher who I love with a passion.

We met at uni and have been inseparable ever since. He is also starting a new job, ironically with the police as a graduate entry. He hopes to become a detective one day and I think it's an honourable thing to do.

So, here we are, right back where it started and I'm taking a moment to accept that this it, my moment of reckoning.

"Excuse me."

I turn and see an elderly man holding a folder in his hand and he smiles warmly. "Good morning, I'm Keith Wickham, the chairman of the local neighbourhood committee. I just wanted to welcome you to Meadow Vale."

"Oh, hi, I'm Lola."

"I'm pleased to meet you, Lola, are you moving in alone?"

He looks concerned and I smile. "No, my boyfriend will be here after work."

He visibly relaxes and says with interest. "What does he do, work that is?"

"He's training to be a policeman and I'm a junior lawyer."

He chuckles and I wonder if I've said anything funny. Then he smiles as a woman around the same age as him, arrives by his side. "Honestly, Keith, I leave you for one second and you're already chatting up a beautiful young woman."

He smiles and as I see the look they share, it melts my heart. They're in love.

The woman holds out her hand and says sweetly, "I'm Verity. I'm married to Keith, and between me and you, we're newlyweds. We've just got back from our honeymoon in Scotland."

"Congratulations."

I smile because they look so happy it's infectious and then Keith says with interest, "You should meet Jasmine, she's a lawyer, a good one at that. You would have a lot in common."

"I'd like that."

Verity nods with enthusiasm. "Why don't you settle in and maybe drop round tomorrow evening to meet the rest of the neighbours. They're a lovely bunch and will be pleased to have a new face to gossip about."

They share a laugh and I feel a warm feeling inside. This is what I wanted. I knew I'd find it here.

The couple move off and I hear her whisper, "Are you going to tell her what happened in that house?"

"Shh, Verity, you know we don't talk about that, the poor girl would have nightmares."

My heart quickens as I turn back to the pretty pink door and hesitate, the key shaking in my hand.

For a moment, I stand and collect my thoughts before I insert the key in the lock and the door swings open. I swallow hard as I see the familiar staircase, although now a soft grey carpet feels comfortable against my feet. Nervously, I start my tour of a place I never really got to know. The kitchen, the living room and the little study set in the furthest corner, all seem alien and unfamiliar.

My heart pounds as I take my first step up a staircase I thought I'd never see again. The memories swirl around me like a dangerous mist, and I'm unsure what I'll feel when the fog clears and reveals the terror of my past before my eyes.

As I turn the handle on my old room, my heart quickens and I shut my eyes tightly as I'm transported back in time. Will it be the same, will it break me?

As I step inside, I just see a light and airy room bare of any furniture and just the shutters to remind me I'm in the same place.

As I move across to the window, I have a flashback to the time I waved my red t-shirt and look at the gardens of the houses opposite. They are more established and there are even two trees that weren't there before. I wonder if the people that lived there are the same? Maybe they moved on, maybe they stayed. It will be interesting to find out.

There is one more room I need to see before I can say I've faced my fears and the nightmare is truly over.

"My heart beats frantically as I approach the room of my worst nightmare and the scene of my lowest point in life.

When I turn the handle of the room I feared most, I step inside and feel—*nothing*. I have no feelings at all as I look at a room that is nothing like the one I left. Bold wallpaper decorates the once bare walls and a bright blue carpet covers what was once bare boards. There is no furniture, just a newly installed set of mirrored wardrobes and as I look around me, I feel finally free.

It's gone.

The memory, the pain, the suffering and the self-loathing. This is now my house of new beginnings and I knew I would find peace here.

A knock on the door makes me jump and I think back to the last time I heard it.

A little nervously, I head back the way I came and answer the door, seeing the removals man on the doorstep.

"Is everything ok, love, would you like us to move the stuff in?"

Flinging the door wide open, I positively beam at him. "Yes please, I can't wait to get started."

Yes, I'll be happy here - we'll be happy here because this is where my path in life was determined. I always wanted to be one of the people who lived a happy life here. Now I am and I will make it the happiest, most successful one I can.

The End

NOTE FROM M J HARDY

Thank you for reading Behind the Pretty Pink Door.

If you have enjoyed the story, I would be so grateful if you could post a review on Amazon. It really helps other readers when deciding what to read and means everything to the Author who wrote it.

Connect with me on Facebook

Check out my website

READ ON FOR MORE BOOKS BY M J HARDY

ABOUT THE AUTHOR

Have you read?

Learn More

The Girl on Gander Green Lane

The Husband Thief

Living the Dream

The Woman who Destroyed Christmas

The Grey Woman

THE GIRL ON GANDER GREEN LANE

Have you read?
The #1 Bestseller

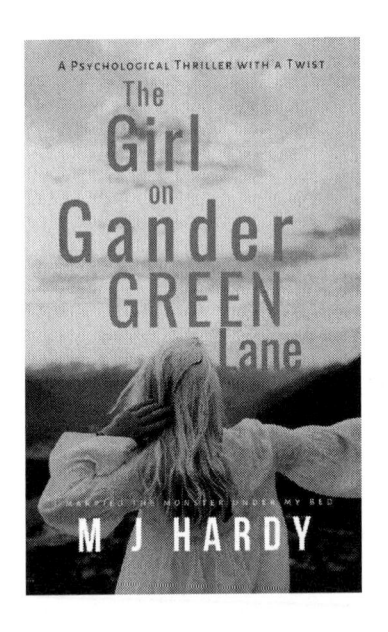

THE GIRL ON GANDER GREEN LANE
BLURB

A Chilling Psychological Thriller with a Twist.

When a perfect marriage, the perfect husband and perfect life is nothing but an illusion.

Then one night, the nightmare reveals itself.

Sarah Standon is living the dream, at least that's what everyone tells her.

She is the wife of a successful solicitor who looks like a movie star.

They live a Stepford existence and appear to have it all.

But then one fateful night, everything changes.

A terrible accident leaves Sarah alone to deal with a situation so frightening that she starts to question her grip on reality.

Her perfect life has been exposed as the lie it always was and she loses everything.

She thought that was the worst that could happen.

She was wrong.

The Girl on Gander Green Lane

THE HUSBAND THIEF

Have you read?

THE HUSBAND THIEF BLURB

How well do you really know your husband!

When Tom Mahoney was mugged on his way home from work, they thought it was the worst thing that could happen.

They were wrong.

When Tina & Harry found out they couldn't have more children, they thought that was the worst thing that could happen.

They were wrong.

When the new teacher Isabel Rawlins arrives, she brings with her a secret that's about to blow their respectable worlds apart.

Five lives all intertwined and heading on a collision course.

Will their relationships survive, or is one or more couple about to find out there's a husband thief in their midst?

Remember, if you have trust, you can conquer anything. When trust goes, madness sets in.

This tale comes with a twist it's doubtful you will see coming.

The Husband Thief

LIVING THE DREAM

Have you read?

LIVING THE DREAM - BLURB

Have you ever wondered what it's like to have it all?

Four couples live a charmed life behind the security gates of an exclusive development. To everyone else, they have a dream life. Beautiful homes, designer clothes and more money than sense.

Behind closed doors, the story is very different.

Beauty is skin deep and when you scratch the surface the blood runs cold. Betrayal, dishonesty and lies are about to blow their worlds apart and not everyone will survive.

Who is telling the truth and who is hiding a secret they would do anything to protect?

Money doesn't buy happiness; it buys a more expensive kind of trouble.

When your friends are your enemies in disguise, expect things to get ugly.

Living The Dream

THE WOMAN WHO DESTROYED CHRISTMAS

Have you read?

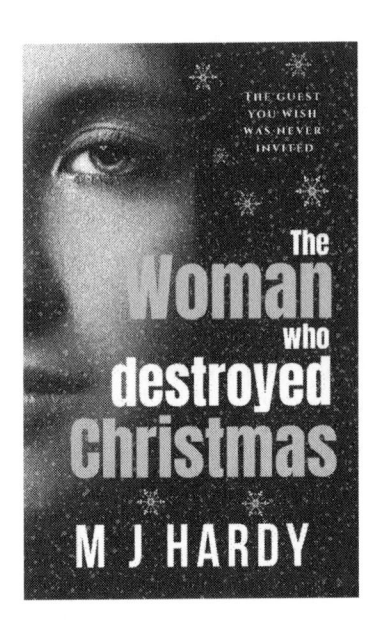

THE WOMAN WHO DESTROYED CHRISTMAS - BLURB

How far would you go to protect your daughter?

When Alice Adams met her daughter's boyfriend, she was far from impressed. He was everything she didn't want for her little girl and so decided to give fate a helping hand.

Luckily, they were invited to spend Christmas with his family which was just the opportunity she needed. Three days to ruin their relationship and save her daughter from a lifetime of regrets.

However, Alice has secrets she hopes her daughter will never discover. In interfering with fate, she unlocks the past with devastating consequences.

As the snow falls and the sleigh bells ring, this will be one Christmas they will all want to forget. There are more than presents under this Christmas tree and as they unwrap the past, the future will never be the same again.

Alice Adams thought she was prepared this Christmas – she was wrong.

The Woman who Destroyed Christmas

ABOUT THE AUTHOR

Thank you. I feel very fortunate that my stories continue to delight my readers. The Girl on Gander Green Lane reached the number 1 spot in Australia in the entire Kindle Store. The Husband Thief and The Woman who Destroyed Christmas reached the top 100 in Canada, the UK and Australia.

I couldn't do it without your support and I thank each one of you who has supported me.

For those of you who don't know, I also write under another name. S J Crabb.

You will find my books at sjcrabb.com where they all live side by side.

As an Independent Author I take huge pride in my business and if anything, it shows what one individual can achieve if they work hard enough.

I will continue to write stories that I hope you will enjoy, so make sure to follow me on Amazon, or sign up to my Newsletter, or like my Facebook page, so you are informed of any new releases.

With lots of love and thanks
Sharon - aka M J Hardy

Ps: M J Hardy is a mash up of my grandmother's names. Mary Jane Crockett & Vera Hardy. Two amazing women who are sorely missed.

Printed in Great Britain
by Amazon